CW01082986

WATCHING MRS GORDON
and other stories

BY THE SAME AUTHOR

Winter Journey

WATCHING MRS GORDON

and other stories

Ronald Frame

THE BODLEY HEAD
LONDON SYDNEY
TORONTO

For my mother and father

British Library Cataloguing
in Publication Data
Frame, Ronald
Watching Mrs Gordon and other stories
1. Title
823'.914[F] PR6056.R26/
ISBN 0–370–30680–5

Printed in Great Britain for
The Bodley Head Ltd
9 Bow Street, London, WC2E 7AL
by St Edmundsbury Press, Bury St Edmunds
Typeset in 11/13 Ehrhardt
by Inforum Ltd, Portsmouth
First published 1985

Contents

'Tragedy' first appeared in the *London Magazine*, 'Excavations' in *Scottish Short Stories* (Collins), 'The Tree House' in *Introduction 8* (Faber), 'Secrets' in *Punch* and in *Introduction 8*, 'Other' in *Fiction Magazine*, 'Piccadilly Peccadilloes' appeared in *Introduction 8* and was broadcast on BBC Radio 4; 'Paris' appeared in the *New Edinburgh Review* and in *Scottish Short Stories* (Collins) and was dramatized on BBC Television; 'My Cousin from Des Moines' was broadcast on BBC Radio 3, 'Watching Mrs Gordon' on BBC Radio 4, 'Thicker than Water' on BBC Radio 3.

Tragedy

In front of me, on the wall, I've got a pinboard stuck with whatever I could save. Candy wrappers and a Giorgio price label and tickets to a gala at the Ambassador and a dolphinarium show at Laguna Beach. I stole a menu from Ma Maison once, and I've a Park Drive packet with Katharine Hepburn scrawled on it.

Down one side I've some of the stills the publicity people sent me. When I look at myself I can't really recognize who it is. Late 1978, into '79, you had your hair crimped and even in Hollywood you wore what everyone else was supposed to be wearing. Maybe it was a little different, just: the yellow clingtop had to be a bit tighter and better cut, the designer jeans were Calvin Klein and the Jourdan shoes — all heel and straps and nothing else — were too impractical for mainstreets.

Most of my shoes were from Feet First on Olympic Boulevard: the big stars spent ten thousand dollars every visit, Mendel took me there because it was good I should be seen and perhaps he thought some of their luck might rub off on me. Streisand and Minnelli had the shop closed if they were coming. I was small-time, but you've to think big: you stay small-time unless, like your agent always tells you, you push yourself right in there and hustle. They were nice places to hustle, but getting out of that life was the best thing I ever did.

Ottawa isn't everything — and I hate the winters — but it lives, a little, just enough: there are good shops, a few places to eat out. It warms up at night, and I look down on the plaza lights. They're quick at getting the snow off the streets, and this apartment has electric under-floor heating. I live off commercials now — and Canadian commercials at that — which was the last thing Mendel ever wanted for me. What *he* wanted, though — I don't know why I give myself that unnecessary drag on my conscience.

* * *

It was Mendel who took me out there. He'd seen me in London in a Poliakoff play about a student and his dress-designer sister who share a bed for a night. He told me I made myself look devilish — maybe he said 'demonic' — in a very, very sexy way: neither of which I'd really intended or could have thought myself capable of.

He followed the 'sexy' line, delivering me things to wear that would show how very little in fact I was wearing. It was like a story for me, the movie director sitting in the audience, reserving the same seat every night for a week. He told me his head was always full of people he was putting through their motions, but none of them would have faces. He'd cradle mine in his hands as we stood at the back door in a dirty draughty corridor waiting for his car to come.

I need to explain for my own sake: it didn't give me any of the pleasure I pretended, that, the physical bit. He was too old for me, or what I thought was too old: fifty-five, sixty. He had a silvery goatee beard and he was bald except for some long strands at the sides and back which were dyed an even, too shiny black. He'd the olivey sort of Jewishness I wasn't very much used to. There was something, I could feel, wrong about us from the start, which anyone could have seen: his six foot whatever and the camel coat that made me think at first he must be an impostor, and my naiad, petite Englishness, sharp high-set cheekbones and chilly grey eyes, puckered mouth, fair flyaway hair summoned up and into a bun like a ballet dancer's. He made me out feyer than I meant, all English reserve, immobile features straining sensitively not to express anything so vulgar as feelings.

Once we got to Hollywood, none of that mattered. Our oddness got us noticed. We flew in for New Year. Plastic fir trees rotated in shop windows and children were skate-boarding in

Bermuda shorts and t-shirts along the sidewalks. A Howard Johnson inn on the long drive out had 1979 beamed in fluorescent green the height of its services tower. Everyone at the airport, in the limousine, was being as nice as they could. Englishness, I'd read in a *Time* article, was very bankable, and so I tried not to let it impress me unduly. I like to think that now, from the safety of my Ottawa winter, how cool I was, how well I handled it.

At least, let me say, I was better prepared for it than I might have been. Within a few days I'd met the trail-blazers — Jane Seymour, Jacqueline Bisset, Lesley-Anne Down, Jenny Agutter, Lynne Frederick — and I kept my frosty distance from them. Mendel told me I'd be bigger than all of them together.

There and then I didn't see why I shouldn't believe him. It was his life. If it had happened just how he'd meant it, I would have been galactic. He'd the authority of — maybe (I'm guessing) 80 per cent — financial success for his seventeen years in Tinsel Town, and that was as good a credential as any for someone like me. There was no reason I could see why I shouldn't trust him. *Spook* had picked up a couple of technical Oscars in '77: I remembered watching the awards programme in the Bayswater garden basement or wherever I was, Mendel going up twice and the cameras holding on the other directors in the audience who were clapping their appreciation and respect.

I told him I'd seen it and he laughed and said it was awful, everyone pretending what they didn't feel. It just happened to be him, and it didn't mean anything more than that. They would have clapped a chimp. A chimp in a tuxedo who would carry itself and not crap on the floor and who could smile nice.

He sounded very disillusioned sometimes, but I never really doubted his faith in me: I just had a feeling about it. Him, me. I buoyed along on that most of the time, waiting for what was going to happen. I knew it was going to happen.

We went to little arts movie theatres a lot. He started discussing things with me, how he would have done this or that in a scene. I couldn't always follow. He liked provoking me gently, so that I'd speak up for the director of whatever it was we'd seen; at these times I was confident enough with him to argue little points back — when I thought he was being unfair — and he tried to make me think we really were having a dialogue that could confirm things for good or bad in his mind.

That felt great. It wasn't quite the same when we were at home, in that pretty San Fernando imitation of a plantation owner's house — all green shutters and white pillars that echoed hollow when you tapped them and a second verandah upstairs that didn't feel quite as secure as it should. Every so often I'd get the odd sensation the proximity wasn't really that at all and we were only getting further away from each other. I sat watching television for hours on end, till that bored me more than his silences. I knew he had a new film to think about and that for once, even with 'Louis Mendel' on top of the credits, the money wasn't going to be easy. That accounted for me, I thought, because it was the film which had brought me out: I'd be girl six, Jacqueline Bisset's understudy's understudy, the English Rose he needed for the script who finds herself in Manson country and haunts herself to death. I couldn't make very much of the script, but I'd remind myself it was Hollywood and it was Mendel, so what the hell.

He tried explaining it to me. He wanted 'to go Chabrol': up-market, sophisticated, which meant arts theatres. I knew he needed the money too, though, he was too used to the bible truth of paydesk returns, and I could see what he wasn't telling me, that he was caught between the two. In the end the money, as he'd anticipated, was only four million dollars, and it depressed him. I told him I'd have done it for nothing. He said no one liked the script, he gave me their objections, it was too glib-smart, phoney-clever: Bertolucci meets Godard: his audience didn't want European philosophers, existential chit-chat: he should cut the flashes forward, back, the confusion about whether the girl is actually there or not, and alive or already dead out of fear.

I tried to brighten him up. He had everyone against him; I thought I could be sorry for him. Even that wasn't very easy. Merelle, his wife, phoned up from Chicago one day and I answered, and she started shouting all sorts of things down the line, not about me, but about him. Through the crackles I could make out what a life it had been for her. I just thanked her politely for phoning, asked her if there was any message I could give, and she slammed the phone down on me.

I didn't say to Mendel about Merelle, but it made me want to get closer to him. Not physically, because I was awkward enough about that. I suggested places for dinner, and we went. We drove up the coast, to Pismo, Vallene, Morro Bay, we found little rocky coves and stood watching the breakers, catching their spray. It was all oddly stilted, standing there and saying nothing. I'd turn round and he'd be looking at me the way he'd looked at me in London the first night he took me out, plaguing inside me for that she-devil he thought he'd been watching on stage. He wanted me, I knew, to be something more, something more than I was, but I couldn't work out what. I felt the evil in those narrow starlit coves sometimes.

It was much better when we just drove. Drove and drove. He had a white Porsche, and we got up to 140, 150. We listened to tapes, over and over. There was one particular tape we both liked which we couldn't stop playing. Everything then was Bee Gees music and he had me pick up 'Spirits Having Flown', which was very new, and we blew the quiet sea roads listening usually to that. That music's like the perfect distillation of blandness and I could have listened to it for ever. He had a machine that turned the tapes over or ran them back from end to start, and we didn't have to do a thing except sit low in those white leather bucket chairs and listen.

Slowly, through the songs, the film became clearer to him. Eventually his words were like a kind of counterpoint to those orgasmic harmonies. I could listen to them both together, and I didn't have to distinguish. Hearing him speak soothed me as much as the overproduced melodies did. I was helping him — very indirectly, I imagined — but I *was* helping him (it pleased me, I suppose, to think it; it made some sense of all this time we spent night-riding). I was just feeding him the final few clues he needed, straightening out the last knots and tangles. I remember one night, he stopped the tape and played the gunshot or thundercrash near the end of 'Tragedy' over and over and over again, concentrating very hard. Every time the voices wanted to soar, he cut back, got the shot or the thunder roar. We almost skidded once on an uphill and the wheel arches on my side grazed on the sea wall, he seemed so obsessed by it.

He even liked the name and asked me what I thought about it for a film. *Tragedy*: he tried fitting it into sentences, as if critics had been talking about it or someone was asking for a ticket at a box window.

'The new Mendel movie, *Tragedy*.'

'One reserved Late Show for *Tragedy*, please.'

'Do you think *Tragedy* will come to be considered a prime example of the genre?'

And here are the nominations for Worst Film: *Planet of the Apes Revisited, Tragedy . . .*'

'*Tragedy*,' I added, 'was Sara Peploe's first major Hollywood film, and one, even in her later days of superstardom, she never quite forgot.'

I remember saying it. I remember him watching me so strangely. He looked spooky-eyed in all that darkness. It was as if he had the she-devil in the car with him and he was frightened suddenly what he could be made to do. I shivered a little and pulled my coyote jacket tighter round my shoulders. Sometime after that we pulled into an empty gravel-park behind a boarded hamburger shack and he put the tape back. He started asking me for things he hadn't wanted before. I didn't want to do them. There were only the stars and the cold light off the sea and he looked older with all that silver shining in on us. I wasn't saying anything and he got more impatient. After a bit I told myself I hadn't any choice in the matter and tried smiling. I caught my ice eyes in the door mirror as he tipped my seat back and he began telling me all over again, how I was going to be bigger than any of them, more than I could ever know.

* * *

We started shooting in late May, in the empty cream-panelled rooms of an abandoned Empire villa we'd stumbled across a few miles inland from one of those forgotten clapboard fishing villages we haunted in our phantom white Porsche.

Mendel had been sure enough about it to have his lawyers get him a rush lease. I though it was very elegant, very decorative, but it left me cold. Even on those days when the California sun stales the blue out of the sky, and lunchtime's like a knife slicing between the eyes. An elderly, very rich attorney had built it in the 1890s as a gift of health for his beautiful, mad French child-wife. She tried to set fire to it, because she'd forgotten what love was or because she was too young to know, and because even a palace can seem, to the wrong turn of mind, like a prison.

I could feel that communicating presence in the rooms from eighty years ago, and I hated it. There was another person watching always, worse than the camera, and I could hear her silks swishing as she retired into the corner shadows to witness. There wasn't any real break to it because it was all locations this time, and every day had to be got through. I was a bit unhappy anyway with having to say less and less and then just acting out silences. If I could have thought about my work even, but Mendel seemed resolved I wasn't to have that saving dignity.

Most of what was shot was me in various states of enticing undress. I wore a lot of georgette and satin camisoles — more than one girl could ever possibly have — tiny black chiffon tops over black silk slips cut very high, red and green stockings slung from suspender belts, rhine-stone shoes from Feet First with no straps and thin pencil heels, stiletto boots from a speciality warehouse in Bellflower. A London girl from Michaeljohn in Beverly Hills drove out every day and did my hair. We would joke about things and that helped a bit.

Really, I couldn't understand what was being expected of me. There wasn't very much plot left after Mendel had blue-crayon'd his way through it, and more or less all I had to do for four weeks was either stand stock-still as if I were petrified by fear or run panicking from one room to another to another. In some shots he got me to take my hands and pile up my hair we'd been an hour dressing or I'd have to throw my weight over on to one hip so that my legs looked longer and the camera couldn't ignore my pelvis. He'd ask me to look blank and usually I could oblige easily enough. Waiting to retake some particular silence, I used to wonder if it was going to be a porno movie and he wasn't telling me. There was some nude stuff later on, but he made them night scenes: the crew he didn't need were sent home. I had to exorcize myself at one point, and I found that the worst embarrassment, the things I was meant to do. I pretended I didn't understand, but Mendel was very patient with me. He seemed to know it was a kind of game, having to explain everything three times over: I liked to think I had my integrity, my reserve left, it was like we were walking circles round each other, it wouldn't have done for either of us to come too close.

* * *

We still had our night rides — in spite of everything — a hundred miles sometimes, more even. Some compulsion in us both wanted those unlit, twisting ribbon roads up to Guadalupe or Surf, parking the Porsche and picking our way down on to the rocks, listening to the sea singing in the caves. One night I slipped and Mendel grabbed for me and when he'd caught me he screamed in my face that I could have killed myself. I was shaking, sick because he was shouting at me and calling me names; I don't know where I got the words but I started shouting back, it was only because he'd money on me he cared anything: I was an investment and he needed his return, his guaranteed percentage and sod him if he thought that was the only thing which still kept me in the place.

I don't really know what I meant. I wasn't telling Mendel I loved him, because I didn't. I wasn't in love with my own ambition: I'd had too many disappointments, promises that had gone bad on me. Mendel looked at me in that same strange crazy way he always did, as if I could defy him to something he wouldn't be able to understand. He frightened me like that, just staring, the thoughts left open between us.

Nothing more happened. We got back into the car and roared off, I forget where. We had nothing else to say and the cabin throbbed with the Bee Gees and the ricochet of pistol shots and those voices piled on each other pushing up and up through the roof.

*   *   *

A week later I'd almost forgotten. I'd finished my part in the film and felt relaxed for the first time in weeks. My being so cheerful sent Mendel into a worse depression, but suddenly it seemed to clear again — over one night — and I told myself maybe my life could work some good after all.

And then some time after that, while he was racing through the cutting, it was my birthday. I got a card from Miami from the Bee Gees, and I couldn't really believe it when I opened it. I've got the card on my pinboard, but it belongs to a different woman's life. That was the best birthday I ever had or could ever have again. We'd a party and everyone came, lots of people he wanted me to meet — Warren Beatty, Vitas Gerulaitis, Cher. And then at midnight — like Christmas morning — Mendel whispered me out on to the drive and nodded his head across to the garage where a mechanic in overalls was taking a cloth to a shining black smoked-glass BMW coupé.

I couldn't take it in, any of it. I gave Mendel a vague hug and he started kissing me, covering my neck and the tops of my arms. We walked over to the car, very slowly. I ran my fingers along the paintwork, enchanted. People had come out and were watching us, shouting things. I wanted us to be alone, I didn't want it to be another performance. Mendel wouldn't stop kissing me — the insides of my ears, my mouth, my wrists — and I felt embarrassed and tried to shake free. He fumbled with a shoulder strap and nuzzled closer into my neck so I couldn't concentrate. It was as if he was meaning to make sure they all saw. I guess that's how it must have been. He needed them to remember that moment, store it up against what was supposed to follow.

For me — apart from that little part of it — it was the best night of my life. We drifted back inside and I let myself be drawn upstairs. While we were away I'd the feeling things beneath us were beginning to get a bit out of hand, and I could see Mendel was distinctly uneasy when we came back down. The rooms smelt sickly sweet, how rooms always smell at Hollywood parties. I picked some poppers up off a mantelpiece and virtuously tossed them in the grate. Something happened outside — someone passed out in the pool — and there was a tremendous panic. Someone else fell through a window. About four there was a fight in the garden and I tried to keep Mendel away from it. Merelle had told me about his heart, and I didn't want an emergency to have to cope with by myself. He said he felt responsible, though, and we had to go out and see. We reached the door just as someone was revving the BMW to life and went squealing off down the drive behind the sweep of gardenias.

Mendel staggered out and blew up in a blind rage. I'd never seen it before, even when things on the set were at their very worst. I couldn't really understand if it was happening now, my own perceptions were so out of sync. I watched him standing on the steps, yelling at everyone he could. For some reason I was involved in it, and when he came back in he pushed me out of his way. He snatched a phone from a magazine man when he heard the word 'police' and flung it across the hall, catching a girl on the arm. The girl screamed, and he threw her some bitch line about her kind in the movie world.

I kept away. Everyone left, and then in the morning — about nine or ten — there was a call to say the BMW had gone off the road some place south of Big Sur and the police were coming over. I persuaded Mendel through the bathroom door he had to see them, and he came downstairs. The police told us it had happened on a blind bend, a woman coming up had seen it: the car spun over, the back seemed to lift up and then it had slammed into the wall and the driver got thrown out. If the wall hadn't been there . . . : the sergeant explained, it happens all the time on that sea road, the car just rolls over and over and smashes itself down on to the cliffs. They were interested that the car was so new. I told them I'd never even driven it. They said someone had looked at it and they were presuming the propshaft snapped: probably the bolts hadn't been tightened properly or they'd managed to work themselves loose somehow.

* * *

I don't know when it clicked, that day, the next day, next week. Not immediately. I was too shocked and saddened. It had something to do with realizing Mendel had never once said how glad he was that it wasn't me.

I couldn't prove anything, of course. I could have put the police on to the mechanic. I simply asked Mendel, when I'd got the courage up, did you try to murder me? He just looked at me how he would look at certain moments, stunned by something that seemed to live inside me which only he could see. I asked him again, did you try to murder me? He didn't say anything, and got up and walked out of the room.

I moved out that morning and a real-estate office found me a very smart apartment in a block with security guards behind Wilshire, eight hundred dollars a week. I mailed Mendel for the first advance on the rent. I phoned up another time and got the answering service and told him I wanted to see him, saying where and when — I didn't leave my name. He was in the restaurant when I arrived, huddled in his camel coat, and we had a dignified enough conversation. He looked sick. I told him what was half-true, trying not to see him, that I'd something else set up and I wasn't jeopardizing it. I gave him the prepared words. *Tragedy* wasn't going to come out. I'd be bigger than even *that* would have made me — 'that', I was leaving it unstated: the big news 'fatal accident' story, which would have been on every tv screen and then made me top box office in Los Angeles and across the country for maybe five or six weeks. I wasn't, I said, damaging my career for his pride's sake. He leaned forward to touch my hand and I pulled it away. He told me what I knew, speaking very slowly, that the film was over-budget now, and that left him with five million dollars owing: he had to get it back. I looked at him very hard and pronounced my words clearly: in that case he'd have to find another way, wouldn't he? (In my head I was calculating what the insurance pay-out on me might have been: a million-and-a-half, two million?) He pulled up the collar of his coat. He seemed to be shivering while the fans whirred overhead to keep out the lunchtime heat. He muttered something about no one being able to prove anything, and I reached for my bag and asked the question, how many registered BMW mechanics did he think there were in Hollywood? What's good enough for me, I smiled at him getting up to go: I meant it as a very private joke that would just be between the two of us . . .

* * *

I opened accounts on Rodeo Drive and had Louis Mendel billed. One afternoon I spent two and a half thousand dollars in Feet First, and because I was last customer of the day they closed the doors. Somehow a letter reached me from Merelle in Chicago, and she said she'd seen me on 'Hollywood Squares'. She wrote again after she saw me on the national news when Mendel's house was burned to the ground and they did a biopic on him. We spoke to one another long-distance and we sounded like loving widows reunited in our grief.

Tragedy's still in the can. Mendel had a copy in the house and it was among the very little stuff that survived the blaze. They said on the news it was hundreds of degrees centigrade at the white heat core where the fire began and the tenders couldn't get close enough for almost an hour. The *Tragedy* coincidence was a godsend for them, and they played on it. The fire chief said the garden was like a tinder box. Even the Porsche got burnt out, I discovered later. I went back to check things, the little I could. The same afternoon I went over I had my luggage taken from the apartment and put on a flight to the first place that came into my head, Ottawa. I caught the next plane up and in eighteen months I haven't been back.

* * *

Spook's on at a local movie theatre, I noticed driving home yesterday from a Fabergé promotion in a downtown store. There are always these funny little reminders in the day. I've tried listening to the Bee Gees again, and it's strange, that even helps me. People see it and they think I'm just pleasantly dated. There's still something so soporific and so excellently mindless about those songs, it could have been a dream. It wasn't quite, and I mustn't allow myself to get that way.

I've got a pinboard to tell me it happened, while I want to remember, but things have a way of working themselves into corners and then off the board into drawers. I've a closet full of shoes but, like they say, you can have sixty pairs of shoes and you've only two feet to wear them.

If there's anyone knows about applying yourself to the here and now, it ought to be me. By rights I should be in an atomic-proof urn or pushing up daisies in Forest Lawn (if daisies are permitted to violate that velvet turf). I should be playing the movie theatres coast-to-coast six programmes a day.

* * *

Sometimes I listen to that song, and everything's either *before* it or *after* it. That life and this life now. It makes it easy like that, the two don't have to belong. It's just something that happened, and walking out of the block in the morning in the red sun and the cold, I'm smiling the bright, cheese-grin lie that I can live with it.

Excavations

They came to her garden twice a week to dig. They wore duffle coats and bright woolly hats. She sat in the drawing-room, pretending to read her *Times*, watching them: just the tops of their pom-poms as they worked deeper down in the trench with trowels. They'd told her it was a hill-fort, second century, like the ones in Perthshire, in Gask Forest. 'How strange!' she'd said, trying to sound pleased. 'Having it here — under my feet, literally — and never knowing.'

They'd all asked about her late husband, of course.

'Did Professor Douglas excavate any Roman sites?'

'No,' she'd said. Then she remembered, and had to correct herself. 'Yes, he did. Just one. Once, a long time ago. I don't think any more than one, though.'

They'd all heard about him, these brisk, cheerful, thoroughly modern students. Professor Harold Douglas: the legendary expert on ancient Greek-Cycladian antiquities.

Their asking about him and remembering what they'd read in his books, it should have been a comfort to her. Should have been.

* * *

She took them out fortifying Darjeeling, which Mrs Mackie the housekeeper made in a vast enamel tea-pot, the same utensil that had been used when they'd lived in Sussex and had staff beneath stairs. Changed days altogether, having to bring it to the kitchen door herself (Mrs Mackie's back plagued her after years of service in the house, she couldn't cope with loads). Two of the hefty boys — young men, rather — would obligingly run over to take it from her and carry it across.

Wrapping herself up, then going out and talking to them all — it was like the very few times Harold had allowed her to accompany him to a site, long ago at the beginning of their marriage. She'd come to realise he didn't like her travelling with him, she'd thought it must be because she upset his concentration. (Archaeology had still been an unorthodox activity for women in the 'thirties, the famous exceptions notwithstanding. And Harold — with all that was Scottish in him — had been a self-confessed respecter of orthodoxy.) She'd come to appreciate too what hard work it was: often when Harold was on a dig, labourers would be brought in to do the initial shovel work, under his supervision. He told her they could be 'uncouth', 'rough-and-ready', and she'd presumed he kept her from them for reasons of delicacy.

* * *

Harold, her husband, had been a very fastidious man altogether. Fastidious in his dress, in his physical mannerisms, in his philosophy of aesthetic 'taste': and in domestic matters too, the houses they lived in, and what they ate and drank, and whom they employed as staff. He was concerned to know the social degree of the people they might have for their friends, and he told her it was right that they should be so concerned.

Harold had been fastidious and discriminating in his overall superior attitude to life. She'd never blamed him for that, of course not: she wouldn't have expected or, more importantly, *wanted* the situation to be otherwise. He was the man she had married, after all.

* * *

They'd met in 1934, at a house-party in the Oxfordshire countryside. She came from a local landed Cotswold family (her father was an Honourable): Harold Douglas was a young Scotsman at the University who already had a considerable reputation as a Hellenic archaeologist — in those days one of the respectably eccentric occupations for young men of good family who couldn't decide on a proper profession.

She'd treated it that first afternoon almost as if it were a pastime. It was her wry smile and an arched eyebrow that brought them into each other's company, separated him from the fawning crowd of his young fellow-students. 'You think I'm not serious, Miss Wentworth?' he asked her, in a Scottish brogue that was strange to her and charmed her. He was blushing as he spoke to her, as if the proximity of a woman (and one noted for her prettiness) unsettled him, or simply because he'd lacked occasions in the past to become familiar with her sex.

She apologised to him — and smiled properly.

She discovered afterwards he wasn't quite as she imagined — at least his background wasn't. His father didn't have the funds to hand which would allow him to subsidise a son's eccentric endeavours, however respectable they were. Harold was having to earn the money himself, in his spare time, any way he could. He told her that on their third or fourth meeting. On the same day she also learned that his father was a minister, he lived in a dour Banffshire manse; he was a widower whose pride in life was having brought up not one but four sons, without ever having been required to ask the aid of any woman.

* * *

By that time — when he had the confidence to admit such things to her — Harold Douglas was being invited to her family's house as a weekend guest.

His behaviour under these new conditions (which intimidated so many of his fellow-guests) was irreproachable. He seemed remarkably at home too in the castellated pile, the Wentworths' seat, built as stout and imposing as a fortress. He admired the lawns, the strutting peacocks, the ha-ha, her handsome brothers.

Quite suddenly it happened, with no warning — during their seventh meeting — he proposed to her, in the gazebo.

'Yes, I shall marry you,' she said, not allowing herself to think twice about it.

At that time in her life all she'd really been sure of was that she didn't want a Wentworth society wedding, being married off (as seemed expected) to one of her brothers' hearty friends. But she had believed too that she admired Harold Douglas — for his intellect, for his seriousness. Also, he had dark, chiselled, Hollywood good looks.

Thinking her decision over in the days and weeks afterwards she persuaded herself, really he was as close to good-enough-for-perfect as she was likely to find, and she should start considering herself a very fortunate and contented young woman.

* * *

They lived in Cambridge first of all, in a little steep-staired house near the river that always reminded her of an old, creaking ship. Students trooped into the tiny panelled hall from the street and went clattering up and down those stairs like ladders. Some days and most weekends Harold went off cycling with them to inns out on the fens to discuss their work with them.

Then they both upped sticks and moved to London when, at thirty-five, Harold won his professorship — from a crowded field of well-qualified candidates. But she was more often alone in London than in Cambridge, because now Harold had his evening lectures in Bloomsbury to deliver, which didn't bring him home till eleven o'clock some nights: and also — a more significant development — he had restarted his programme of Greek research, which soon was taking him out of the country, to site excavations in the baking white land of dust and lotus flowers he called his 'spiritual home'.

Four or five times she accompanied him to Greece: or, more exactly, she followed him, she took the train out to Athens and stayed at the Hotel Grande Bretagne till he'd finished and could join her. He made a point of not asking for her company at the places where he was digging, and she didn't intrude; she presumed he had his own reasons, that he knew best. In noisy, humid Athens she filled her three or four weeks of blue-skied loneliness as usefully, as culturally as she could.

* * *

During the War, it was better. Harold was invited into one of the Intelligence departments, and he worked office hours based in Guildford.

He had to travel down and back up on an ordinary red bus. She liked him at that period for his new social ease, which was something she hadn't expected to find in him: it also seemed to be suiting the more egalitarian times they lived in. He might repeat to her snippets from conversations he'd had on the bus with servicemen, about their experiences. She enjoyed that; she was anything but a snob herself.

* * *

Almost at the end of the War, an old buzz-bomb which exploded opened up a crater a mile and a half from their elegant house in Kensington, and underneath was discovered a treasure none of the experts had suspected was there: a temple to Mithras, the Romans' god of the sun.

Harold was involved as an adviser on the excavation work. As the temple began to take up more and more of his time and attention, she sensed she was encountering the first serious testing she'd had in her marriage — overlooking the Greek absences and her sojourns in Athens. On three or four evenings of the week he would go out and leave her to her own devices; the explanation he always gave her was that he had to make sure that the place was being properly guarded from prowlers and vagrants. People's morality was all upside-down these days, he never failed to remind her.

She knew it was true, that 'morality' *was* in a state of flux and couldn't be depended on. There did seem to be less trust generally in the world: despondency and privations made ordinary people greedy. You only had to open your eyes and ears to see and hear. A new homeless breed stalked the blitzed areas, camping rough on the rubble flats; in Battersea and Pimlico unexplained bonfires lit the sky at night; from Barnes to Lambeth packs of dogs ran wild, she could hear them baying from her chintz bedroom next to his. Churches had fallen, dragging their bell-towers; banks had had their roofs and walls blown away, and stories abounded of paper money scattered like leaves in the streets. Nowadays the most innocent-intentioned people just going about their business weren't spared either: there were new dangers lurking, the ground was riddled with treacherous air pockets into which you could disappear in a split second, with only a scream left behind you.

That was how they were living. Topsy-turvy, upside-down.

He would come back home to her at the end of his day, looking terribly drawn and tired.

'It's only a temple,' she told him once.

'*Only?*'

He had given her such a look of incomprehension it quite frightened her, ran dead man's shivers up her spine.

* * *

The War stopped. Confetti speckled the streets. Pink ribbon hung in the trees after the Victory celebrations.

As well as the War, Harold's teaching stopped too — every subsequent spring and summer as a rule, sometimes for the interval of a whole term. He left her then, to go off to his sites. It became a ritual and a duty with him, and he ceased justifying his excursions to her. For private reasons she couldn't define to herself — she experienced it more as an instinct — she felt less inclined now to pack her suitcases and follow him. So she didn't.

Dutiful letters and postcards would arrive from Kythnos, Samos, Ikaria, from wherever he'd gone. They were politely affectionate but they told her little about the place and the work. Often — on the 'letter' days especially, when she either received or wrote one — she wished she had a child she could make a proper home for, to take her mind off her oppressive creature comforts and the perfect good taste which (quite unlike the dullness in other people's lives) she was fortunate enough to be surrounded by.

A child, however, to further grace their existence, with a share of his father's good looks and her blue blood: that had most definitely *not* been Harold's wish.

* * *

Curious things happened when she was left on her own in the Kensington house. The maid would come sprinting upstairs and tell her so-and-so was waiting down at the front door.

'Show him in,' she would say.

'He's not quite . . . that kind, ma'am.'

She would go downstairs herself. The eight or nine times it had happened over the years she'd found a man standing on the top step. Quite young, but not at all like any of the *soigné* students who came. Each time it was a different man, but they all had physical similarities which linked them. They would be rough-looking, badly-dressed, unshaven. And — she couldn't help noticing — they were each of them handsome, in a brutal, rather animal way. They would ask to see the 'guv'nor'.

'I'm sorry,' she would say.

And explain: Professor Douglas was at work, or he was out of the country.

Her lady's vowels had them tipping their caps. She would mention to them the Mithras temple or the other London sites Harold had come to have charge of afterwards. She said the word 'security', and they would nod their heads back, but with a puzzled expression. She didn't know if they understood, if they were quite capable of it. Wasn't that why they were here? — they were men without jobs, they wanted to be site-watchers?

The maid didn't like her to have more than a few words with any of them, and would push slowly on the great front door to signify that the exchange was over.

She didn't think to tell Harold about the doorstep visitors, incidents in themselves very trivial, when he called London long-distance from Greece, on an expensive, crackly telephone line.

* * *

In the blind and ironic way Fate operates, it was the telephone that was the instrument of their joint undoing.

Not till many years later when, to make their quiet domestic life still smoother-running, they installed one of the early Ansafone machines.

Harold was in Greece, on Kos, when she came home one day and switched it on. There was only one message; the tape played back a man's whiney voice — a youngish, American voice — asking for 'Harold'.

'Please — I wanna see you.'

The voice also called him 'Harry', which *she*'d never done, wouldn't have dreamed of doing. Harold wasn't a 'Harry', not to her. She was mystified. The voice left no number, and just rang off.

She was in the house one afternoon when there was a call and she answered. The man — she recognised it was the same man, the American — asked for 'Harry'.

'My husband, he's not at home,' she told him — rather grandly.

'I'm broke,' he said. 'I've gotta get some money. Quick.'

'I'm sorry,' she repeated. 'Professor Douglas isn't here.'

'Tell him . . .'

'Who *are* you?' she asked.

'Johnnie.'

'Johnnie Who?'

'I was on a dig. In Mykonos. You know? *Mykonos*.' He said the word with an odd, jokey sort of emphasis that also sounded very knowing — unpleasantly so, to her ear.

'He flies home on Sunday. I shall tell him you called,' she said. And put the phone down.

I certainly will *not* tell him, she thought. What on earth could his not having any money have to do with Harold? And how rude and familiar he was.

She forgot to tell Harold about 'Johnnie-Who' in the excitement of having him back. (She was always glad to see him home, her husband with his aloof, matinée-star good looks.) When the phone rang that first Sunday evening and she picked it up and she heard the American's voice, she just didn't want to be bothered.

'Look, just tell him . . . ' the man said.

She did, and she held out the receiver at arm's length. Harold, burnt by the sun but dressed again for winter in his well-cut Shetland tweeds, took it from her. She made a show of leaving the room, and left them both to sort the confusion out.

It must have been settled, because she didn't hear about it again — and she didn't dare to involve herself in 'business' and ask.

* * *

The next summer — one fateful morning she never forgot — she was in the hairdresser's reading an American magazine a girl in a mini-skirt had left behind when she picked out the word 'Mykonos' from a page of print. It was an article on travel destinations for 'swinging singles'.

> *Try Mykonos — if it's your bent! — but be warned. It's the chic-est, swing-iest, gay-est Greek island there is! Seeing the bars at night is believing! Exquisitely tarted-up 'queens' rub bronzed shoulders — and anything else! — with young bank clerks fresh out of the closet . . .*

Sitting there roasting under the drier, something awful occurred to her. She felt quite queasy and sick.

Later, safe home in the bathroom, she leaned over the wc as her stomach heaved and a little jet of bile came spurting up into her mouth.

* * *

Even after Harold died — in his sleep, in his bedroom in their spacious and secluded Sussex home, the most respectable of deaths — she got telephone calls. Without Harold there to intercept them on the study phone, she had to deal with the garbled voices and their unintelligible messages by herself. It was why in the end she'd left Cuckfield and moved up to Scotland — to escape. (His 'hame links' Harold had romantically called them, but his Scottishness was an accident in that respect, it hadn't had anything to do with her choice. The sprawling Edwardian seaside villa with its green roof and garden pergolas and well-stocked rose beds had been the first desirable-looking residence she'd turned to in the estate agent's plush brochure.)

She lived elegantly in her Fife home (didn't she deserve that, to be comfortable?), but she wasn't very 'social' any more. Her circle was much reduced. She'd stopped — it was the worst consequence of all — she'd stopped *trusting* anyone Harold had known. She would remember at moments in the day all those students and fellow lecturers (the youngest and most personable of his colleagues anyway) she'd had to entertain to tea, whom she'd made up picnic and punting-supper hampers for. In the early days she'd been helping to subsidise Harold's work with her share of the Wentworth money (there were standing arrangements at the bank) and she'd tried so hard to be a willing hostess too — all to advance *him*, for the sake of his career — and she had thought nothing of arranging lavish luncheons and formal dinners for six, eight, ten, afforded out of her own ample funds. Sometimes she'd invited pretty and eligible young women of her family's acquaintance to join the party and brighten things up — she saw Harold didn't like to say 'no' — but those evenings when she had other female company never worked well: despite her best intentions, they went hopelessly flat. Harold seemed happiest when there was only herself to represent her sex, sitting at the other end of the table the maids laid with her share of grandmother Dufellis's silver, and when he had his favourite squadron of handsome disciples flanking either side.

* * *

That was in the 'thirties. In the 'forties and 'fifties too, and even later than that, the students used to attend in dinner jackets. Now — she watched the young people outside her windows, enduring the perishing east coast cold with their red noses and mittens and merry bonhomie — it was different.

So much was different today. Maybe Harold — if he'd been

starting out now — he wouldn't have married; he could have done it on grants? Maybe, though, she *had* given him something he wouldn't have had otherwise? More than just the confidence of money which her inheritance had allowed them, although it was certainly connected with that. They had been quite a famous pair in their day, after all, in their prime: while they were sensibly sparing in its use, people had agreed that together they possessed — rarest of qualities in the world now, in the stark, depressed, sceptical 1980's — *glamour*. They were already the photographers' darlings in *Tatler* by the time Harold won his chair at London.

* * *

Now someone in Oxford — that beautiful honeystone city of lost causes — was writing a book about him. A young go-ahead don apparently, with his own reputation to make: the most dangerous kind, as she knew from experience.

He hadn't phoned up to arrange an interview with her. Would he? — would he do her even that simple courtesy? She was pretending to people — those of Harold's old professional peers who still kept in touch, the less physically attractive ones whom she had far less cause to shirk — that she knew nothing about any book.

What would it reveal, for God's sake?

All the hours of the day and night her head was filled with the worry of it — like a heavy dark stone placed there. (Or — she sometimes imagined of those niggles of fear when she'd drunk too much of Mrs Mackie's tea — like little scorpions which would never be done snapping at her.)

At least there were no children and grandchildren to shame. And — it gave her bleak comfort to think — she would be dead herself in another five years, in less time than that in this harsh salt wind climate.

If it could only be kept from her that long . . .

* * *

She'd heard a horrible rumour, on the academic grapevine, from a student of long ago who claimed he had contacts in Oxford, at the Ashmolean. It was what made her unable to concentrate on anything — *The Times*, 'Woman's Hour' on the radio, the diggers outside.

It was going to be a 'modern' biography, evidently. To do with 'the man'. Like his excavations, it would 'get beneath the surface'.

Her source had written to her in his letter, he had it on very good authority that 'no holds will be barred'. Also, he told her, the title was going to be an archaeological pun. She understood from what he said that the choice was already sending little shock-waves pulsing through Academe. It was intended to be a serious joke, the title that would move the books off the shelves in the shops double-quick, in no time.

It seemed that the title would dictate the 'marketing slant'. The publicity men, who worked so far ahead, they liked it. They thought it was a winner.

The best ideas — wasn't it said? — are always the simplest.

The title inhabited her, like a haunting thing.

The words they'd settled on (neither the best — nor, she knew, quite so simple) kept blazing in her head, writ large, a-glow in scarlet and flame.

'FEET OF CLAY'.

The Tree House

They were walking down Drayton Gardens, the two of them. I saw them from the other side of the road and stood behind a tree tying my shoelace till they'd passed. I was perched on one leg, shaking. They disappeared into a block of mansion flats.

I placed myself behind another tree and stood watching as the lights went on in a room on the first floor. I narrowed my eyes as she walked over to the balcony doors and looked out. He was pouring drinks at the sideboard: I could just see the tops of an armada of bottles. He handed her a glass and she took it without looking at him. Maybe he put music on because she started moving her hips. She was still watching the length of the street. Could she have seen me? But if she was hoping for another look to confirm it really had been me, she gave up soon enough. She pivoted on her high heels, swinging round in her silks to give herself to whatever domestic life they lived now like tamed savages in the quiet heart of Chelsea.

We were children together once. There was Alan — and Claire — and me. I think Alan — and Claire, by complicity — were the evilest people I've ever known. Were, are. (I didn't even think of ourselves then, when it happened, as *children*; I didn't make that prime mistake of presuming we were innocent. A child is an adult without any softening social graces — but given an intensity of character which the years seem to take away from you. That intensity can be terrifying. At the time those two filled my perspective as fully as any grown-up did.)

Our families lived in a small Wiltshire town with an abbey, famous for its picture-postcard looks. Alan's father was a senior partner in a law firm, and did court work in Winchester; he was well known for the sharpness of his brain and won all his cases (even, it was said, when he had the proof his client was guilty). His wife was his only failure to date. She'd done an unheard-of thing: she'd run away. I heard my mother and her friends discussing her, exchanging the rumours — someone thought they'd seen her (or her double) attending in Harrods' haberdashery; and because they knew her mother lived in Hove, another time they decided she'd fled to Brighton for a gadfly life and she'd already been disgraced in some unmentionable way. Claire's father was the second-in-charge at the abbey, and decency personified; her roly-poly French mother feelingly played Debussy on the piano at amateur concerts fund-raising for the roof. My father was a doctor; my mother was a scion of ancient, inbred pedigree stock, she raised me (rather tiredly) and belonged (indifferently) to the West of England League of Lily-Growers and had afternoon bridge sessions in the house when she could summon the energy to spin the dial on the phone to muster her friends. This only matters set against the truth of our three characters, what our lives had made us: Alan — pushy and masterful like his father in the courtroom, impatient, unscrupulous, unforgiving; Claire — sensitive and thoughtful and conciliating like her decent father, but in the end fickle and weak; and me — I don't know what, nothing very much, careful, hesitant, testing, uncommitted, and at the mercy of them both.

We were supposed to become friends simply because we lived in genteel houses on the same pretty street. But the houses dated back centuries and were built like little palazzi, fortresses with high stone walls the colour of saffron and railings and gates and hedges, and for all we normally saw of other people's existences we could have been living fields apart from them. There was also such a thing as a residents' association, recently got together to keep Foss Street pretty and in the 'right hands' and to judge on the colours of front doors, and I can see now that really our intended 'friendship' so-called was just a consequence of that inspired gesture of adult self-interest.

My mother invited Alan to our house one day, a few months after his own mother's flight. She prodded me on the shoulder when she introduced us so I'd take him outside into the garden. (It meant I was to be 'nice' to him.) Claire, who was my friend already, looked as embarrassed as I was feeling myself. The three of us played Grandma's Footsteps — 'What's the time, Mr Wolf?' — but Alan was rather rough about it and had great delight catching us both. Claire and I had to sit down by the little pond for a breather.

It was Alan, standing over us watching us, who suggested it — out of the blue. 'We'll build a tree house!' Claire said she'd never heard of a 'tree house'. I'd seen a photograph of the bush hotel on stilts where Princess Elizabeth was staying in Kenya when she became Queen and I thought of that. He decided the first fork on the old oak would be ideal. He ran back with us to ask my parents. They said 'yes, of course', with kindly smiles to compensate for Alan's motherless condition.

The tree house took a few days to build. It also gave Alan unlicensed access to my garden. At the weekend my father found us lengths of wood he hammered together to make a platform, with four more planks for a balustrade on each side. (Banging away, he told us there was a tradition of having bedrooms upstairs in houses because our ancestors, the cavemen, used to make *their* sleeping places in trees to be safe from predators. 'Animals?' I asked him. 'Yes. Or humans,' he said.) Claire contributed some lopped branches from a pine tree in the vicarage garden: they still had their needles attached, and Alan without discussing it arranged them to make a chalet-style roof to give us shade. My father knotted some chandler's cable-rope to one of the other branches. Then it was more or less complete and ready. Claire's mother gave us two tins of condensed milk and a packet of Playbox biscuits to fortify us. We thought the biscuits were a bit juvenile: we were seven and would have appreciated digestives, or ginger nuts, which are harder and you can nibble at longer.

We had the 'opening' one afternoon when my parents were out and the help didn't see me removing the soda syphon from the sideboard. Claire squirted it at the trunk and said the proper words, gleaned from abbey fête-openings. I followed Alan's lead — but less earnestly — clapping and whistling. Then we each shinned up the trunk. My shoulders strained with the unaccustomed exercise. When we were up the three of us sat down, but awkwardly. There was something not quite right. It wasn't just the seasick feeling: maybe it was because the planning and anticipation were over and we realized this was what it had been in aid of and we didn't know how to begin. Claire smiled sweetly at us, how her mother smiled on her charity musical evenings. I smiled too — in the vague way my mother did when she welcomed her professional bridge friends to the house. Alan didn't smile. (Was it because he'd forgotten how *his* mother used to smile, I wondered — if she ever had?) He just watched us; he wouldn't stop looking at us, his eyes flicked between us. Claire had phoned me up about the pine branches in her garden without letting him know, and I thought he must have taken it as a slight. Much more than that, I can appreciate now — it had been read as a deliberate cut, a prearranged snub, an insult, a scornful challenge to his kingship. That was Alan. He could always imagine things were any number of times worse than they really were. Sitting there cross-legged his anger seemed to be consuming him. I was fixed by the pull of his eyes. From her to me, me to her, her to me, me to her. (Was it a habit he'd picked up from his unhappy parents, when he sat witness to the public-room silences like adjournments between their prosecution bouts upstairs we used to hear with our windows open, which my mother called their 'blow-outs'? You couldn't be sorry for him, though: Alan wasn't like that. I knew that even my expertly diplomatic parents could only spare him their tender smiles, not their sympathy. Already at seven he was ringed with barbed wire; his eyes hooked into you, tore flesh.) I think that for something so very little — Claire telling me first about the axed branches instead of him — he hated me.

I don't use the word lightly. My mother always forbade me to say it. 'You dislike something strongly . . . ' she would correct me. I'm not sure what the difference was: maybe it sounded more elegant and less raw, put that way. But Alan didn't just 'dislike strongly'. Hating is a trait of paranoia, it fixes on the object, it belongs to an obsessive nature. His mother's days — until she abandoned husband and son — had been spent keeping the house as antiseptically dustless as a space capsule: in the evenings she would have to lie down in the bedroom with a migraine and that's when the famous quarrels began. That's how it began with Alan too, the inherited oddness, and then his father telling him (when she could hear) that his mother was off-the-beam.

The anger happened again about something else. I was used to the talk of my mother and her friends about that mania for cleanliness and order driving Alan's father to a frenzy — so now their home without anyone to look after them was reputed to be a midden of unmade beds and unwashed dishes. After several visits to the tree house, Claire started in like vein. She announced in a lecturing voice that we ought to have a 'system' about things: for instance we should scrape the mud off our sandals before we climbed off the rope. She insisted the biscuits should be kept *there* and the lid must always be put *tightly* back on the tin. Alan was hating it, his eyes flared at her. I took her side, by instinct I suppose, and said we needed 'discipline'. He told me very quietly — but spitting the words at me — to 'sod off'. He must have heard his father use the expression to his mother. It was new to Claire and me, although it sounded angry and we could guess its rudeness from the tone. I was feeling that incidents like this could only make the two of us closer, Claire and me (even when we weren't *meaning* to hurt him). Alan was smart enough to spot the intrigue (if that's the word for it) starting for himself. Claire — patching up — asked him to open one of our two precious tins of condensed milk with the tin opener. He saw through that ruse. 'Ask *him*,' he told her, his eyes tightening on me. 'You can have one of your own,' she said to placate him, with a new energy and desperation in her voice. But he wasn't listening to her and got up and swung off down the rope. (He was easily the best at that. He'd seen a Tarzan film on television. Neither of us — see how I make the association? — neither Claire nor I in our separate homes were allowed to watch television as indiscriminately as he did.)

'Anyway,' I shouted after him, stuck for anything else to say, 'it's *my* garden.' It sounded crass and stupid and the words seemed to float in the air without going away. He walked over and started to jump up and down on the rope, drumming his fists on the boards of our floor. The house rocked, like a boat on waves. Claire screamed and clutched my arm. 'Please, please tell him to stop!' I didn't want to tell him any such thing. He kept thumping his fists on the planks. 'Oh, make him stop!' I didn't know what to do. I couldn't let him get away with the outrage, but I realized things were just about over between us and I wanted it to be all *his* doing, not mine. I was determined. (Can you be determined at seven? Why not, as at twenty-seven or seventy-seven?) The raft of planks we were standing on began to tilt. The blows shuddered up through my legs. Claire was in tears, waving at him. 'Please stop, please stop! *Alan*!'

And it stopped. That was all he was wanting her to do — say his name. I shut my eyes, opened them again: I'd thought I was going to be sick with the motion. In a moment he was perfectly gentle and he was helping her to slide down the rope. She was shaking and had to lean on him. I blinked at the two of them as he entwined his arm through hers and they walked off together across the lawn, through the haze of summer insects.

Another afternoon there was a domestic mix-up: I was supposed to be going to Salisbury with my parents after lunch, but something happened and we stayed at home. I climbed up into the tree house, which my father had made safe again, and called at the top of my voice over the orchard into Claire's parents' walled garden. She was outside and heard me and did a Red Indian whoop. 'Tell Alan!' I cried to her. Claire whooped and shouted 'Alan!' in the other direction, but her voice wouldn't have been strong enough to carry that extra distance. I think I knew that when I asked her.

I'd never tried these jungle calls before (the information came from Alan, watching Johnny Weissmuller on television). But I understood straightaway what the significance of this novel method of communication was, that the weakness of Claire's voice gave me an excellent means of excluding Alan any time I didn't want him.

So Claire came on her own and we had a pleasant afternoon up in the tree, out of sight of the house. We chatted and compared our shadows slowly lengthening on the grass towards the pond. We lay on our backs and looked up into the roof of pine branches and listened to the lazy hum of insects under us. We must have started to doze because we were invaded before we seemed to understand what was happening. One moment tranquillity and contentment with our day, the next Alan was flying off the end of the rope and the tree house was an echo-box. 'A-*ha*!' He stamped a war dance with his bare feet, laughing at the shock on our faces. He was dressed up like a crazy pirate. He had red stuff like lipstick smeared on his cheeks and a curtain ring over one ear and a bright yellow towel for a cummerbund. 'Well, well, well!' It sounded just like his father talking to his mother, when his voice used to travel to us on a still night and before she packed her bags and ran away. He pushed on my chest with his foot so I couldn't get up. 'Well, well, *well*!' He kept saying it, smiling down into my face. But none of this was meant to be fun.

He bent over me and dragged me across the platform by my arms. I tried scraping my heels on the floor like brakes then twisting my bottom from side to side to slow him but nothing could have succeeded against his strength and purpose. My head was suddenly hanging over the edge with empty space underneath. 'Well, well, *well*!' He wasn't laughing any more. Claire called to him to stop. He told her, 'Shut your mouth!' Then I seemed to be back inside again, on all-fours, and he was booting me in the bottom chanting, 'Out! Out! Out!' Claire had her hands on his shoulders. 'Please don't, Alan! Please don't!' He flung the rope at me: I held on but I was shaking like jelly and when I slithered down it went burning through my palms. I fell on my back on the grass and the pain made me start to cry. Alan had landed behind me and was yelling at Claire to come down. He grabbed my arm and began to pull me like a dead body. I saw where he was making for, the pond. 'Go on, take his legs!' Claire came running after us. 'What are you going to do?' 'Take his legs! Do as I say or I'll throw you in too!' I don't suppose she felt she had any choice and she tried to lift my weight; she couldn't and dropped my legs and then picked them up again when Alan said he would twist her arm. He called her a 'bloody woman' and she burst into tears at such foulness. She let me go and Alan pulled me the rest of the way, quicker so he didn't lose this opportunity to do what he wanted to do to me. I believe that at seven years old he had the badness in him to know I would be his revenge on the world.

As I tried scrambling up off the flagstones, hands pushed into my aching back which sent me pitching fowards again. I could hear screams and shouts from my mother and her bridge friends who'd seen. I crashed into the water and the cold was like splitting ice. My eyes opened and I seemed to be tumbling through space, passing stars. My arms must have floated up and the rest of me too, for after the blackness I was on my back seeing a blue summer sky shining absurdly far away from me. The branches of the tree were like cracks in a blue plate. Then between me and them I saw two faces peering down, the crazy pirate's, and the one behind with a wondering look. Out of the sky two arms came reaching into the water, but not (as I thought it must be) to save me. They seemed to want to hold me down, not help me up. The striped face dropped closer, and at one point I was making the connection, that the arms belonged to *him*. Alan. His white hands fluttered above me like sea anemones in a swell. I felt them fastening on my neck and I tried in the coldness to find them with my own hands. I locked them on something but I didn't know any more if it was him or me. I'd gone down and bobbed up again and my head must have made a hole in the water because I could hear the panic of high voices. I think I went down again — or twice more — before there was an explosion of water and through it other arms were reaching in to rescue me. I felt a different kind of strength in them, and I gave myself willingly.

They lay me on the grass and it was what I saw when I could open my eyes to observe the world — the tree house — above their heads, beyond their concern, where the clouds seemed to have torn to fleece on the oak's branches. It was riding the afternoon very precariously. A sudden wind might bring it down. My mother saw me looking. 'Daddy'll repair it,' she said through tears and she tried to make me more comfortable till he came, brushing off insects with her scented handkerchief.

If he does repair it, I was thinking, I live in it alone this time. I saw afternoons ahead, and books, and biscuits, and watching into people's rooms and never being seen. For a moment, with the sun finding me through the grid of branches and warming my face, I seemed to be picking wisdom ripe out of that blue air.

Piccadilly Peccadilloes

She was fifty before her life really began. She'd made a lot of new friends since their move to Abinger. 'Never mind forty,' she'd tell them, making ripples in that quiet pool.

Only a certain amount was known about them in their new Surrey circles. Charles had retired from his job early, that much and no more was divulged: 'FO. Foreign Office. Here, there and everywhere.' (Someone even went to the bother of checking: it was all bona fide.) They had no children: 'I don't think it's a life for them, not really, do you?' She said that coming here was just a beginning, she realized that her life after all their postings had many other possibilities left for her. (Other than what exactly, she didn't specify in any more detail.) Her new friends nodded wisely when she added that now for the first time their lives were their own and naturally, having waited for it so long, she was going to make the most of it.

Her candour didn't altogether stop the speculation. It was her friends' opinion — and the reason why she attracted and kept them — that she lived very grandly for their means: she wasn't privy to these remarks, though, whispered rather guiltily after her prodigal lunch parties had dispersed, and so happily she remained none the wiser. Of course they were right and wrong, her friends, as people always are about that kind of thing: top-flight Civil Service pensions aren't inexhaustible (there was more checking), but as she'd explained so often, for her it was like another life just beginning — 'out of our grey period', she liked to say, making an arty joke of it.

*

At fifty, the magic age, she learned to drive. The other wives made do with rusty, hand-me-down Morris Minor Travellers, and brows furrowed when a high-performance, electric-blue Alfasud with fat tyres and tinted film-star windows appeared parked anyhow in front of the shops. 'My gad-about,' she called across to the warden, beaming at him and driving off before he had his slip completed.

The garage was informed through Mrs Perry that her husband wished to open an account; she told her confidantes she hated this sordid business of paying and having to appear knowledgeable about pumps and nozzles. She hinted they'd been used to things being done quite differently, she and Charles. The word got round later that it was the gardener's boy in the end who had to do the necessary. (The gardener's boy — two pairs of hands now in the garden — like the car and the front gate that swung back automatically and the sunken patio in the old rose garden, another extravagance much discussed of late in the more genteel domiciles of Abinger Hammer.)

Her favourite days, though, had nothing to do with Abinger or, properly, with Charles. 'His golf's enough for him,' she liked to say, making suffering faces.

No one saw much of Charles, least of all at the golf club: his port-wine nose and his jolly laugh collecting the papers in the morning had been welcome additions to the local scene when they came but all too little in evidence now, the husbands complained: too much of her and not enough of him. She repeated that she went to London only to get away from golf talk and locker-room jokes: so her lunch guests smiled with her and nodded because no one really knew positively what went on of an evening once the chintzy curtains were drawn across the creeper-fringed leaded windows. (Lunchtimes, oddly, were her social hour — a professional legacy, someone suggested vaguely — and Charles to the general disappointment declined many more invitations than he accepted.)

'Oh, yes, I need my lovely days up in London,' she said very mysteriously. 'Again.' ('Again' in case her friends would forget she'd had another life before the one before.) She claimed it was an excuse to dress up: dress up *more*, she meant, because she'd set new standards for Abinger. 'Treats keep you young.' No one felt they could dispute the wisdom of *that.*

Two or three times a month it happened. She always took the Alfa. Driving gave her the illusion of somehow managing her own destiny. She parked at the underground car-park in Berkeley Square. Knightsbridge bored her now with its circus of tourists, wops hogging the pavements as if they bloody owned the place. 'Horrids,' she called the shop to her friends, who were impressed and shocked together by her occasional disrespect for seasoned customs.

After all those years away which she wouldn't be drawn on, she'd fallen into a routine surprisingly easily. Her morning began the way she liked it to begin, sipping a cup of coffee and eating a warm flaky croissant in the quiet of the Westbury Hotel coffee lounge. When she'd used the ladies' room she made a graceful exit through the front doors and headed straightaway for Bond Street.

She thought if anything *it* had improved with the years, unlike so much else. She sauntered up one side and down the other and remembered how she'd walked it with Charles in their salad days. She stopped at the windows, sighing at the pictures in her head till she felt they were starting to trouble her. She wouldn't let them trouble her. She had her favourite shops — The White House, Asprey's, Elizabeth Arden, Rayne — and she knew she only had to walk inside any one of them to lose the memory. This was her own world. She felt she understood its magic. The names themselves were like a kind of spell. Pinet, Régine, Celine, Ferragamo.

She took her time and when she'd finished and seen all she wanted — perhaps even indulged herself in a pair of shoes or a silk square — she braved the traffic on Piccadilly and beetled off to Simpson's. She enjoyed telling her friends it was her favourite shop 'absolutely anywhere'. She loved its spaciousness and the cool white marble floors and stairs from an age she'd never known. When they were living in their backwaters she'd thought about it a lot; in Accra or Nicosia or Aden (she forgot which came before which) it had seemed to become everything she was being kept from. Now she could walk upstairs with her hand on the shiny steel and imagine she was Nancy Cunard or anyone else of that set with their mad, quicksilver lives she'd spent her years reading about. She loved lingering at the rails and she loved the shop's flattery of attention, the solicitous assistants scattered about each department anxious to help and no pains spared: that sort of service, like the décor, didn't seem to belong to this dismal age she'd come back to with its mania for sameness and impersonality. Sometimes she didn't want to leave and she'd spin the time out, choosing between one jumper and another or trying on the Daks skirts; the skirts had a clever way of making her look even thinner and narrower than she'd already disciplined herself to be.

After Simpson's it was lunchtime almost. She dropped into Hatchards and did a round of the fiction table and then quickly upstairs or downstairs according to her mood. She liked looking through the art books; just occasionally, though — it was against her better judgement, she felt — the intensity of the other people alarmed her slightly and then it was a relief to be back outside again on the street. Over-much intelligence was something she felt it prudent to be suspicious about.

At twelve-fifteen she checked her watch and swept up the side stairs into the Ritz. The pink carpets and snowy marble always dazzled her till she could adjust to it. She sat on a stripy sofa in the bar and ordered a Tropical Dream. She fished three crisp pound notes out of her bag to include a tip. There was always the same handsome wavy-haired barman in a white apron, and she laid the three notes down separately on his tray. He'd started speaking to her the last few times, nice day, how was madam. She'd overheard his name was George. 'I think that's a lovely name, so English,' she ventured one day with a foreign lilt when the Tropical Dream seemed a stronger concoction than usual.

After the Ritz she stepped as nimbly as she could manage across Piccadilly in the direction of Stratton Street and Langan's Brasserie. She didn't like the indignity of being unaccompanied when the *maître* asked how many, but it was less galling than it might have been: it normally meant having to share a large round table for ones and twos which she actually found rather fun. She'd been lucky except once or twice, and she'd met some very interesting people. One came to face-spot of course, those she could after her years in the wilderness — she'd backed her chair into Michael Caine's ankles behind her once — but the table was fascinating in a different way. Catching up, she thought of it, if only to justify some of the expense. Rich Hampstead wives with lecherous gossip and sober-suited businessmen a little uncomfortable with the place and glamorous young people with frizzy hair smoking French cigarettes and discussing pop music. 'I wonder what my Abinger friends would have to say to this?' she asked herself, and remembered timid, mousy wives she'd known in Nairobi and Penang. She effected means of breaking into conversations or starting them: one lunch she was seated beside a rather fey young man who turned out to be a writer, and she told him she was a widow over from Switzerland on a spree. 'I have to fit in Harley Street too. I was advised Lausanne for my arthritis. I was a painter of sorts. You won't remember. The best advice I ever had, Lausanne.'

She liked to hear the black pianist and his Broadway classics, but sometimes the turbot or the artichoke missarda sat a little heavily in her stomach and she thought it better to get up and go. She'd lost the guilt of the first few times and confected appropriate excuses to suit the feel of the day: a meeting with my publisher, my jeweller's resetting some stones, I'm selling at Sotheby's, I've a recital tonight and I need the afternoon to rest.

Weighed down with her bags she moved stolidly off down Stratton Street and between the busy tides of pedestrians on Piccadilly. Soothed by the pianist's melodies she was ready to concentrate for a little while on something more cerebral. The Royal Academy was handy and rarely had anything she felt she didn't want to see: there were retrospectives of artists to rediscover and the summer shows and the big Italian and Dutch exhibitions. (She liked to say she was receptive to it all. 'More or less. Everything except those awful piles of bricks and sand heaps they had in the *Telegraph*.') Occasionally the mental application proved itself just a little too much for her mid-afternoon frame of mind and she'd retreat more quickly than she usually allowed to Burlington Arcade. She'd walk the length of it twice, up and back, and then make her way back across Piccadilly and down Duke Street to the polite frenzy of Jermyn Street. She'd go into Dunhill, lured by the brown plush and low lights; she'd saunter round the cabinets, and the hush and the aisles would remind her what the shops used to be like in New York in the early 'sixties when Charles was still considered responsible enough to go. When she was done and beginning to tire she'd pop across the road to Fortnum's with the little energy left and into the Mezzanine for a seat and a pot of Keemun. She never bothered talking to anyone over tea. She bought odds and ends to take back: mustard for herself and jasmine tea ditto (Charles's taste buds had been the first thing to go), and maybe a tin of biscuits or a fruit cake would catch her eye and she'd start planning an afternoon tea around it.

The rest of her day passed without needing to think hardly. The tiredness crept up from her feet and she found there was just enough to do. Along to Burberry's, read the theatre and cinema bills, then the long stretch back to Berkeley Street. At five-thirty, dead on her feet, she repaired to the Aloha Bar in the Mayfair Hotel and inaugurated the Happy Hour with something Hawaiian-sounding from the cocktail menu. Her thoughts always drifted to what she might do if she actually were a widow. Stay the night perhaps. Take a taxi to Swallow Street opposite Simpson's and order oysters and a good year's hock upstairs in Bentley's.

Thinking taxis put her in the mood and she informed the doorman and was speeded back to Berkeley Square in no time at all. It was much slower work driving up the ramps and out of the garage and around Berkeley Square to get to Mount Street but she had the happiness of her day to divert her and she could even feel vaguely charitable to the other drivers around her. In the mirror waiting at the lights it would occur to her she looked younger than a woman of fifty-two with a not very easy life behind her, and thinking that she'd feel a slow glow warming inside her.

When she got home, of course, it was different. The gate swung back and she'd see from the other end of the drive he hadn't even drawn the curtains. She'd look in the mirror again to set her face properly before getting out. She'd reach into the boot for all her purchases and slam the lid shut to give him warning if he needed it. 'If he can hear even, God help us.'

Inside, every light in the house would be on. She'd find him eventually. The empty glasses and overturned bottles she remembered from a dozen other houses — tatty official residences and then the flats rented for them — would point the way. She'd right the bottles on the tables and patiently collect the glasses together by their stems, rubbing at wet circles on the polished wood with a paper handkerchief from her bag so the daily wouldn't notice. She could hear him usually, blundering about; sometimes he was sleeping; on the bad days the television would be on, turned up very loud, and she was grateful they'd never have neighbours again and all that over-polite hysteria of explaining in pidgin English.

Once she'd found him lying under the piano; another time he was heaped up in the cupboard under the stairs. (Different, she reminded herself tartly, from oleander bushes.) Recently he'd taken to sprawling full-out on the window seat in the sitting-room, a much more dangerous development. He wouldn't recognize her when she came in, and he could only tell who it was when he saw the familiar burden of carrier bags. She'd drop them on the sofa and come across and reach behind him and tug the curtains shut. If he looked as if he was going to suggest anything out of his stupor — what was it costing them, for Christ's sake — she'd kill him with a look.

She would carry on, calmly battering the cushions behind him into shape. She'd say something to pretend it had been a perfectly normal day for both of them. She'd see he was so drunk the words couldn't have come out anyway.

At some point when she was ready she'd begin her delicious little torture, opening her bags and emptying them on to the sofa. Shoes, jumper, blouse, skirt, scarf, books. Travel brochures were a new addition to her list, a glamorous world their missions had never taken them to: the French West Indies, Java, unpronounceable Pacific atolls.

Even if he found them in his soberer moments and could focus his eyes to read, she knew there'd be no serious objection raised. They had the situation, she now felt, understood. It was very simple, although it had taken them a dozen years getting there. So long as she said nothing about his own indulgences, he hadn't the moral authority to say anything about hers. Tit for tat. 'My Piccadilly peccadilloes,' she'd been telling her new friends, taking care they only saw one side of the coin.

She'd arrange her purchases over her arm to take them upstairs, leaving him crumpled with the words unsaid still muddling around in his head. Some day, she didn't doubt, he'd forget and try to say something. Then he'd get it back, what she'd been saving for twenty-five years and trailing round the shreds of the Commonwealth with her, he'd get it so hard he'd feel he'd been blown through the wall. It had never happened, and she hoped it wasn't ever going to. One couldn't be too sure, though. She lived these days on red alert.

They would finish the scene in the same way. She'd stop at the door on her way out and tell him she was tired and could he get himself something to eat. She would explain what there was and where. He never heard, but it was how she was playing it and meant to carry on. Till the alarm bells rang. She'd pause in the hall where he could see, angling her reflection in the mirror. She wondered what he thought, the worst he imagined of her seeing her slim and youthful still: if he drank what he did to tell himself it didn't matter.

'Well, then. Goodnight.' She'd turn her back on him. She

didn't waste time waiting for a reply she knew wasn't going to come. Pulling herself upstairs with her heavy armload of clothes, she was prey to a fleeting moment of doubt. It was just the tiredness of the day, but it was as if the walls were moving in on them and they had water for air. Sometimes she felt a panic of little bubbles in her throat.

She'd pass herself in the wavy landing mirror. She never looked the same upstairs: suddenly she became grim and tight-mouthed. Her skin sagged in strange places. Fifty-two, she'd remind herself, and in front of her she'd see a person turned all to hate.

My Cousin from Des Moines

They didn't come to England till 1962. It was the '*n*'-th year of preparations for a visit that always, in the end, failed to happen.

I'd just arrived home for autumn half-term and at first I didn't believe what I was told — that their plane had touched down at the airport — and I wasn't convinced till I saw for myself the black Humber Hawk taxi come swinging up the drive, axles creaking, carrying its two passengers in the back, one swathed in furs.

'It's your American cousin,' my mother told me unnecessarily, nervous beside me on the top step as we made a little reception committee with my father for our guests none of us had ever seen.

The driver opened the back door of the taxi and my 'aunt', as we referred to her — really my mother's Minneapolis aunt's daughter — divested herself of the travelling rugs. She hazarded a foot out on to the gravel — in a pointy crocodile shoe — as if she were testing the atmosphere. She emerged dressed in a waisted black cashmere overcoat with a fur collar and strange scalloped black kid-skin gloves like hawking gauntlets.

I saw my mother noting again the black stilettos with their red piping. The face we'd never seen was hidden under a broad-rimmed black felt fedora, which I felt none of the women *we* knew in our closed circle would have had the courage to put on their heads.

'Hi!' my aunt greeted us with in a surprisingly light, sprightly voice, unpinning the furs across her shoulders.

A shadow moved behind her in the car. Behind them both the

driver was lifting half a dozen assorted white suitcases out of the boot. My mother drew in her breath.

'It's so cold!' my aunt called to us from under her hat. 'Brrr, I can't take it like this!'

Then she smiled — at the three of us, each in turn — quite charmingly.

My mother relaxed, realising our guest was only being eccentrically American, not insulting.

'Well, I hope you'll be warm *here*,' my mother told her by way of introduction, with just a very little 'tone' in her voice.

I could see better now. Beneath her discreetly black coat my aunt had very long, slender, shapely legs. Behind her, her son — my cousin Walter — ventured unsurely into the hall.

'Unfortunately,' my mother addressed the face under the hat, 'you've come at the very coldest season.'

'Oh, I know I'll be very warm here, I can tell already,' my aunt assured her with another toothpaste advertisement smile, throwing her furs on to a chair like a film star. 'Very comfortable. I've so wanted to see you all, you can't imagine.'

My mother smiled — cautiously — and my father closed the door.

'Do come and have some tea, both of you,' he said.

He was forever at a loss with guests to Oakdene, my father: now for some reason a smile was starting to break on his reserved banker's 'business' face my mother and I were so used to living with.

I examined my cousin surreptitiously while I helped my father carry the cases to the foot of the staircase — while *he* just stood there, doing nothing. He was odd-looking, I saw. He had a triangular-shaped face with a bony cusp of chin, and he was bloodlessly, alarmingly pale. He stood with his shoulders hunched; very arched eyebrows and flat ears set close against his head added to the pixie-ness of his appearance. What made me think him odder still was his not seeming to match at all with his elegant (and, from what I could see, pretty) mother. (How ugly must his father be, I wondered, to correct the balance of heredity?)

He was several inches shorter than I was, although I knew we were the same age (eleven, if the year was 1962.) His height — or his lack of height — was another disappointment, and also his thinness. His hair was like mine, brown, not blonde: it was parted and brushed well off his brow, not crew-cropped. I'd expected he would look like one of the 'Hardy Boys' in the book-cover illustrations: stolid, and assertive, and the very picture of glowing health. Instead the eyes in his pale face flitted among us, like a prying spinster's, missing nothing.

'Did you have a nice flight?' my mother asked, with heroic politeness. 'I can't remember where . . .'

'Oh, we've been everywhere! Everywhere!' my aunt explained, pausing at the hatstand to remove her wide-brimmed hat. She seemed to take off twenty years with it and suddenly I felt they were a generation apart, she and my mother. My aunt pulled at her hair — becomingly blonde (dyed, I think it must have been) and smartly cut — with the tips of her fingers. In her black crocodile shoes and with her black lizard bag and the long kid gloves tucked into the pockets of her coat, she looked very expensive. I was quite fascinated, I'd never been able to study an American at such close quarters before.

'Paris. Como. Rome.' She crossed them off on those creamed, manicured fingers with their scarlet nails. (She was making little perfume trails whenever she moved.) 'Where else, now? Antibes, of course. And we saw a little bit of Switzerland. That *was* cold!'

She walked ahead of us into the sitting-room and made for the fireplace and the crackling log fire.

'Capri. That was just heaven — we spoke to your famous Gracie Fields. And Naples, of course.'

My mother watched her from the hall. 'Of course,' she repeated, just to herself, under her breath.

Their visit to Berkshire was bad timing. We were having a very cold snap, and in another week — when our guests would have gone — it would be November, then December after that, with Christmas fir trees for sale in the village shops. We were to be their last stop before they flew home to Des Moines, Iowa. I supposed we were a family obligation. (The rest of my 'proper' aunts and uncles lived in far-flung spots around the globe, in towns with names I could never remember, so they had no other kith and kin they could visit in England except us.) Or — with the advantage of hindsight to guess from — were we really something else, a different kind of invitation to their travellers' curiosity . . .?

In our sitting-room my aunt seemed very exotic, and rather theatrical: not at all like my staid 'county' mother with her Flora Robson face and scrubbed grouse-moor complexion. For 'housewives', how unalike they seemed! On a scale of prettiness my aunt might have scored seven marks out of ten: she certainly 'made the most of what she had' — as my mother would say of certain women she didn't quite approve of, because (another of her expressions) they 'tried too hard'.

When my aunt took off her coat she was wearing a canary silk suit underneath and fine sheer nylons, and my mother looked most uncomfortable in the other big wing-chair, pulling her tweed skirt over her knees and tugging at the pearls round her throat. My cousin Walter sat, not where he was invited to, but on a hard-bottomed shield-back chair from where he could observe all our different posturings with his range of vision clear and unimpeded.

My aunt burst the seal on a carton of Camel cigarettes and leaned forward in her chair to catch the flame from my father's lighter. I saw my mother taking a suddenly critical view of the situation. Her face set in a kind of social gel I wasn't unfamiliar with as she rang the little glass bell on the table for the maid.

'You'll have some tea, Stella?'

My aunt nodded through the thick blue fog of cigarette smoke. I noticed how speedily her eyes were racing round our sitting-room, as Walter's had done earlier, recording our possessions and seeming to want intimacy with our things.

Like my mother I was already starting to feel not at all at my ease: almost — silly to say — like a stranger here in my own home.

* * *

We'd organised trips for them, planning routes from the AA road maps.

We were always late in starting out, because my aunt would lie soaking in the bath for half the morning, oblivious to my mother's turns of the door handle meant as hints. She would foam the water with flowery scents and the house smelt beautifully for a while, like a florist's, so you really didn't want to leave it. Dressing too took her a long time. She wrapped up well, in layers of clothes: pastel cashmere jumpers and long silk scarves with Paris monograms and coats with inserted wool linings. My cousin Walter always appeared telepathically at the very last moment from his bedroom, looking vaguely guilty, sometimes with his cheeks fired but smothering them in his tartan muffler.

We were out-of-doors a lot that week, so of course it was only sensible to be well-protected from the dampness and cold. We went to Eton and Windsor, and Oxford, and the Vale of the White Horse at Uffington. (We all had to stand in the eye of the chalk horse and make our wish, which my father said would come true before twelve months was out. I whispered *my* wish, to be clever, so I'd get through my December exams. My aunt smiled privately to herself making hers. Walter closed his eyes to wish his wish and started swaying on his feet he was so long about it, speaking softly and secretively into his chest.) We sauntered through fields of amber leaves in the Cotswolds and beside the Thames, which looked like the touched-up stills on BOAC advertisements in travel agents. And all the time I was required (my mother would nod at me repeatedly) to keep my cousin — my sort-of-cousin — occupied, which meant a few glib comments on the weather and patronising explanations of our English customs. These always sounded a bit bizarre as I tried describing them to him, when they'd never seemed so before, hearing about them at school: run-of-the-mill tourist board stuff like swan-upping, the Eton wall-game, Eights week on the Isis, and morris dancing we once saw from the car. Queerly I could feel my grip of the familiar beginning to slip from me, just watching the way he studied everything — in the car, in the house, our tweeds and flannels, my school books, the paintings on the walls, the inherited furniture we lived with, the food we'd eaten for years, how we'd held our knives and forks from birth almost.

I don't think he liked my techniques on these outings very much; I had the distinct impression I was being *tolerated* and that he knew I was being transparent. I wondered what they both said about us, he and his mother, when they exchanged their good-night kisses at the end of the day in one or other's room. My father appeared to bother them least, my aunt chatted and laughed away with him quite happily, maybe with her delight made too obvious to the rest of us. I felt it ought to have been the other way round, that it was *he* who should have been the family connection, because my mother (who was) seemed to have a very limited appeal, like me. My mother wasn't very good normally at disguising her feelings: they had a way of stationing themselves on her angularly English face, like script even the uninitiated could read, brazen hieroglyphics. In this case contentment and joy weren't among them. On our jaunts she sniffed a lot and pursed her lips and pulled at the fingers of her gloves. Her American relations were clearly not to her taste.

One day coming back home in the Jaguar my mother leaned into the front from the back, between my father and my aunt, and turned the radio on. It managed to cover our silence. I remember that the presenter played a record by Jan and Dean. We negotiated the autumnal, switchback lanes in a cold pink twilight listening to that strange music unlike any other, high shiny voices singing of sun and surf and sand. I knew that Des Moines in Iowa is inland, heartland — it's a thousand miles from the sea there — but I heard it as the anthem of our two visitors from the bright lucky land in the west.

* * *

One afternoon when we'd gone to the Chilterns and come back home for a late lunch and my aunt spoke of being a little tired, my mother suggested to Walter and me we go up Windmill Hill, which is really an iron-age tumulus.

He didn't reply at first when I went to fetch him at the appointed time and knocked on his door. I had to wait a minute or two before the key turned in the lock. He'd been lying on top of his bed; the bedspread was rucked. He had a flush on his usually pallid, anaemically white cheeks.

'I hope you're warm,' I said. 'In there.'

'I'm not, very.' His long fingers pulled back a loose strand of hair with a neat, deft movement. (Mother and son, slowly the relationship was confirming itself . . .)

'Oh. I'm sorry. You should have said.'

'You're all too polite for that.'

Too polite?: what on earth did he mean?

'Anyway,' he said, 'I don't like old houses.'

'This house isn't very old. It's Edwardian. That's not very old, by English standards.'

'English standards? I've never been here before, so how would *I* know?'

'I don't suppose you would,' I said, limply.

'Come on, then. Where's this thing we've got to see?'

It was an awful ordeal of an afternoon. I scrambled up the mud slide sides of the scrubby mound in the cold — the 'pudding bowl' it was called locally — and slithered down again, and sometimes he followed me, sometimes not. Every so often when I was explaining something I'd turn round and see he was examining me with his tight, inscrutable eyes shrunk to pinheads. When we walked back down the lane he dug his hands deeper into his coat pockets and withdrew further into himself. I gibbered away. He let me speak, exposing my own nervousness. I wasn't especially so by disposition, it was he who made me like this, suspecting his dark intentions. By a curious and extreme geography of causes, some of the same family blood was swilling around in our veins: that fact had started to alarm me.

My mother beamed falsely at us when she opened the front door on our return. Behind her the log fire sparked in the sitting-room. A bowl of late chrysanthemums sat on the table in the hall, smelling slightly bitter.

'Did you have a nice time, then?'

'Yes,' I said, and made my mouth into a straight line.

In the oak mirror my face looked almost blue with cold; now my complexion wasn't so very different from his, we were even starting to look more alike.

'And you, Walter?' my mother asked. 'Did *you* enjoy it?'

'Sure, *I* enjoyed it,' he said. And smiled. As charmingly as the gesture would have been performed by his mother, whom I could hear (apparently recovered) laughing in the sitting-room with my father. (When had *he* ever been quite so jolly with a guest before, I was asking myself.)

My mother had half-turned round at the sound. I recognised the bath salts perfume from upstairs. Walter walked between the two of us, trailing his coat and tartan muffler and looking saintly.

I followed him. When I was passing the sitting-room doors I couldn't help myself, I glanced in and saw my father and my aunt — my kind-of-aunt — sitting on the sofa, poring over something in *Punch* together. My aunt read out a remark and laid her hand to my father's arm and hooted with laughter again, she said she thought it was so funny. A smile was lighting my father's craggy Scottish face.

My mother tugged at her pearls and told me crisply not to be long upstairs, both of us, tea was almost ready.

I looked down from the gallery upstairs. My mother was still standing in the hall, re-arranging the spray of white chrysanthemums for something to do. She scrutinised herself in the mirror, seeming anxious: perhaps — I'm guessing — wondering how it was that strangers must see her.

* * *

My aunt was a divorcee. Two times over. I'd heard my parents discussing it before she arrived. I don't suppose we'd ever entertained a divorced person in our house, it was a rare condition in those days. As for being divorced twice, that was unheard of, except for Hollywood names in the newspapers.

She wasn't what I'd been expecting at all. She was prettier than I (stupidly) thought someone like that must be. She also seemed in a surer frame of mind than her messy history should have allowed. (But, I remembered, wasn't there a film called *The Gay Divorcee*?) I'd overheard my mother telling someone that my aunt's European tour was at her recent husband's expense and was intended as a mental convalescence, to take her mind off 'things' — but she appeared to me to be treating it very much like an ordinary holiday, without a trace of shame or sorrow. She'd even told us about eligible male company she'd 'met' (my mother in her twin-set sniffing loudly, as if the words had unpleasant depths and I shouldn't be hearing) in Italian hotels and French restaurants. She showed my father how to mix and shake a cocktail she'd learned the ingredients of from a young barman (she called him 'divine-looking') at the Negresco in Nice. She said the cocktail had 'strange properties' and my mother looked shocked. My father adventurously sipped at it while my cousin Walter observed us all from his chair in the corner, his elfin face split by a Cheshire cat smile.

*   *   *

We went to Henley the day after the 'pudding bowl', by my mother's design probably; it was very chilly but it got us all out of the house. My father and my aunt continued to chat a lot, though, and my mother (striding out in her belted tweed coat) walked us farther and farther along the river to postpone for as long as possible the enforced intimacy of the car trip back.

My mother was shivery when we returned to the house and went straight upstairs to bed, with only a squeaky strangled 'goodnight'.

My father took the next day off work and offered to drive my aunt and my cousin over to Stonehenge. Walter pretended to be shivery too, but he let me see it was a performance, a lie. So my father and my aunt went off together, just the two of them, and my mother, my cousin Walter and I, we stayed at home.

Not long after they'd gone my mother got up and dressed and wandered about the house. She looked much paler and less in command than her usual self. The hours ticked away on the ormolu clock in the morning-room where Walter and I were working on a jig-saw. It was a picture of a fox-hunt.

The car lights swept through the french windows from the drive when they got back in the evening. My aunt laughed stepping out on to the gravel. A door slammed shut upstairs. My father's key slithered — a little drunkenly, I thought — into the front door lock.

* * *

The next day, Saturday, my aunt went down with a cold. My father kept sneezing. My mother recovered very quickly — within hours — and started attending to all sorts of duties in the outbuildings and the garden, almost as if she meant the house to be deliberately empty of her presence. In the afternoon she commissioned me to take Walter out again.

'Here's ten shillings, take him to the Marigold Tea Rooms, will you?'

When I opened my mouth to protest, she pleaded '*Please*, dear!' For some reason I looked down at my shoes as I nodded my head.

In the tea rooms we sat at a table for two and I ordered a pot of tea and two toasted Sally Lunns and two almond slices from the trolley. I could see Walter was working up to something, as surely as my mother had been when she sent us out. He sat restlessly, shifting about on his wheel-back windsor chair. The elderly waitress smiled sweetly at us, as if we were both of us little gentlemen.

'Do you like my mother?' he suddenly asked me.

It was like a bolt out of the blue.

'Do I like your mother?' I repeated.

'Well?' he asked. 'Do you?'

'Yes. Yes, I think so.'

'You *think* so?'

'I'm sure I do,' I said.

'You don't *sound* sure.'

'Look, what is this?' I was edgy, as I sensed my mother had been and now Walter was too, in his way.

'I'm only asking you a question. It's important, just to keep on talking, isn't it?'

His hands that had been so jumpy he folded on top of the table and, trying to seem calm, he surveyed the other customers of the Marigold Tea Rooms.

But I knew that wasn't the end of it. I felt I was being compelled to ask what I did next.

'Now it's your shot,' I said, blundering in. 'Do you like *my* mother?'

'I think she must be . . .' His words came out pat, sounding prepared, as if he'd heard them somewhere — ' . . . difficult to know.'

'Difficult to know?'

'Well . . .?' With his girl's fingers he pulled back a wayward strand of his hair.

'Well, what?'

'Isn't she?'

'Maybe,' I said to him. Disloyally.

He sat there recording all the little personal foibles on display at the other tables. He was like a camera.

'My father, then?' I persevered. 'My father, do you like *him*?'

He smiled to the waitress, as if nothing in the whole wide world could possibly be wrong . . .

'Yes. Yes, I like your father.'

A second or two after that — with his gift of impeccable timing — he turned his coy smile back on to me, and this time I felt afraid.

'My mother does too,' he said. '*She* likes your father. Likes him lots.'

'How . . . how do you mean?'

'That's just how she is, my mother. She's like that.'

'Like what?'

'*You* know!'

(I didn't, he knew I didn't.)

'We never get invites to go back again anywhere!' He laughed. It sounded a forced laugh, high, unnatural. 'Boy!'—I felt he used the expression to hurt me — 'the things I've seen!' His fingers lightly, delicately flicked something from his brow.

I cut my almond slice open. It looked as dry as sand in the middle, there wasn't any jam in it.

'Anyway,' he continued. 'I don't suppose we *can* see you again. Des Moines is so far away.'

It doesn't matter, he was meaning, as I tried to fake unconcern and couldn't. *What happens doesn't matter!*

The yellow pastry turned to ashes in my mouth. Why in hell had we been sent here — banished — with the ten-shilling note to spend?

'Do you think my mother's attractive?' he asked. Quite casually, as if he'd just thought of the question and it hadn't been in his head for days to ask.

'Y-y-yes.' I realised as I said it I shouldn't have opened my mouth . . .

'Do you?'

('Attractive' too, why that word?—it was a sitting-room word. I couldn't have spoken of *my* mother to him like that, calling her 'attractive' — even if it had been true, which it wasn't.)

'Do you?' he asked for confirmation. 'Do you think she's attractive?'

Pause. I didn't dare to reply.

'*I* do,' he said.

Another pause. I kept quiet, I was telling myself 'don't speak, don't be tempted, say nothing'.

Then he asked me 'Do you think your *father* thinks she's attractive?'

I jumped up at that, knowing I was only giving myself away. But I couldn't help it. I pushed my chair back and ran across to the door and out into the street, past the flabbergasted waitress. Traffic thundered in front of me. When I turned to look back through the window, he was standing right behind me on the pavement.

'Look . . . look . . .' I blurted at him. 'Just . . . just sod off!'

'That's not nice.'

'Go away! Go *away*, Walter!' Now I was shouting at him. 'P-p-piss off!'

He pretended to look shell-shocked. For some reason I couldn't connect I was remembering his locked bedroom door, the crumpled candlewick bedspread . . .

I ran out into the traffic. Brakes screamed on the road, raw voices floated after me. I raced on, not knowing if it was really me or not: maybe I was a phantom?

Car lights dazzled. Someone laughed, high and shrill. An awful, dire possibility collected among those marble swirls of evening in the sky, which I could see in those seconds stirring themselves into a vast, amassing dark ahead of me.

* * *

In the couple of days that followed it grew and grew inside my mind, the horror: with the evil rapidity of an expanding, giant toadstool. And wherever I turned my head its terrible shadow seemed to be there too — in front of me, beside me, behind.

Even when I knew the harm was safely gone — back home to Des Moines, Iowa, four thousand miles away — I felt there was a kind of poison left behind, it was everywhere and nothing would draw it: it lay on the walls and smeared every surface in the house and made our lives perpetually hazardous. How were we ever going to cleanse ourselves of it?

More days passed. The three of us returned to the pattern of normality, but I felt it was exactly that — the skin, the outer form, a discipline of events that we took on trust. Only that, nothing more.

Half-term was almost finished and I re-packed my suitcase to go back to school. We didn't much discuss our relations, who'd left us a day earlier than I'd expected, my aunt nursing a proper cold at last (the kind that comes on suddenly when the system has received some shock). No mention was made of the car journey on the fifth day of their stay, to Stonehenge or maybe some other undisclosed destination, although I knew it was in all our minds. I didn't refer to the visit to the Marigold Tea Rooms, and my mother kept silent about what had happened in the house in our absence. (Now, I noticed, she had a spring in her step she hadn't had on any of our blustery walks.)

The maid whisked away the remains of the bath salts for her own use. The window was opened wide in my cousin's room to get rid of a peculiar, persistent mustiness; little white spots were sponged out of the carpet beside the bed. The timbers creaked again in the walls and attics of Oakdene as they had done all my life, almost as if we'd had our innocence returned to us and everything could be how it used to be.

It wasn't, though, not quite.

A letter arrived for me from Des Moines three weeks later; it was forwarded to my school.

My mother thinks we should keep in touch, but I've told her Des Moines is the other end of the world. She looked really sorry when I told her.

Anyway, I know you won't forget me. Will you?

Another thing, bet you never got your jig-saw done. I found I had some pieces in my pocket when I got back to Des Moines. It's a long way to post them, so maybe I should keep them. I've got a tree, a corner of the sky — oh, and the fox.

I overheard my mother telling her best friend Lois on the phone YOUR mother sure has a lot of imagination, so perhaps you have it too? And what you haven't got in the picture you can slot the other bits around and make up out of your head (?)

from Walter XX

Secrets

He suspected it was his stomach, but even his doctor didn't seem very sure. He'd kept it from Hilary for as long as he could, but she'd noticed and would ask him in her vague way, why didn't he go to see someone else, a specialist? Whenever he tripped over the word 'ulcer' in a book or a newspaper a kind of despair went through him.

He recorded some letters for the rota secretaries and left the others in the department with their instructions. In the car he felt the usual relief to be out of the building and away from it all, the bright steel and chrome and the Japanese gravel gardens and the rubber plants infesting their floor like a jungle. Someone had shown him a recent copy of *Design* with a feature on well-planned offices, including their own, and his eyes had started to glaze over as he read it.

He took the B-roads back. He hated the obligation of the dual carriageway and had begun to avoid it. This afternoon he was almost enjoying the strange quiet. He told himself it just needed a very minor dislocation like this to be seeing things through new eyes. It was a different race even, passing the cars on the network of humpback lanes after Gerrards Cross, housewives in head-scarves picking children up from school, elderly couples in polished Rovers returning from the shops.

At conferences people eyed him a little askance when they asked him where he was from, and he said Buckinghamshire. Beaconsfield, he would add, and the eyes would narrow back at him. In a way, of course, it wasn't one thing or the other, he knew that: a red-tiled, whitewashed compromise marooned mid-point between country and town. He wondered sometimes how he could explain to them that, really, he was satisfied, perfectly content with the pretty painted shutters and the cobbled walks and the wistaria-hung front their overgrown village smiled on the world. Maybe it *is* a soft option, he wanted to say, but Hilary and I, we're both of us quite happy.

There'd been a time certainly when the very same sort of place would have seemed below his consideration — but only because it was so far beyond his expectations. In the old-fashioned parlance he could respect and understand, he'd married above himself. He would work it into the conversation that Hilary's father still farmed in his Cotswold valley, breeding horses. To get where *he'd* wanted to go all those years ago, he'd had to disinherit himself — at the time the indeterminate mists of suburbia hadn't seemed to him a real background at all — and, he could have added, that's something you don't forget. When he was wooing Hilary, he'd tell her confidently, hoping her father might overhear them, 'I'm never going back there again.'

Another ten years on and here they were, in not so dissimilar territory. He wouldn't have been able to account for it if he'd been asked what had gone wrong in his calculations. Not 'wrong' exactly, and not any one thing, he might have said: it's only what happens to so many people, one's life seems to be fitting certain conditions. Beaconsfield assimilated them both: the prices were on the up and up, they had delicatessens and wine bars on Saturday for lunch, Volvos on either side of them. Their neighbours lived decently and weren't ashamed of their quiet affluence. He had every reason to feel safe.

The knife twisted again in his stomach and he had to pull into the side and rest for a few moments. In the mirror he watched his eyes clouding and the sweat breaking on his cheeks. Hilary, he reminded himself, concentrating on the thought, wasn't to know anything. If she ever chanced to find out . . . His mind wandered, but the possibilities always frightened him so much he told himself 'no' and just let it go.

*

It was a naïvely sentimental thing to think, but it was true: he'd meant everything in his life for Hilary.

They'd met at a hunt ball in Cirencester. When he was at Oxford he'd picked up a curious set of friends: acquaintances rather than friends. Scientists from Surbiton weren't their usual company, and he'd never got beyond the fringes of their coteries, however hard he applied himself. He didn't know enough people in his own right and he could never be drawn on his background — but he'd been tolerated: his looks appealed to both sexes for all sorts of reasons, and learning from that he'd quickly developed the knack of anticipating a person's likes and dislikes and being just that bit more voluble in his criticisms than the rest of the company would allow themselves to be. He was hauled along to hunt balls and point-to-points and regattas and rooftop parties because he could be guaranteed to come up with the withering line, the loud aside, that was going to send the occasion up mercilessly and no one to blame but himself. He bought beige cords and heavy brogues and high-buttoning hacking jackets so that when people asked him what he did and he told them the truth — engineering — they'd look a little hesitant and then laugh, seeing it must be another joke.

Hilary, statuesque and handsome and with so strangely little to say for herself, had been just as uncertain, never seeming to know any better where she was with him. In spite of it, though — or because of it — their love had prospered. On weekends he would take the bus to Astalleigh and spend Saturday night at the farm, adjusting himself quietly to those spacious low-beamed rooms with their ticking clocks and chintz sofas and blue-and-white bowls of pot pourri. Hilary with her empty days became his intimate contact with a lulling, more perfect world, and he came to think of her more and more as its personification and was duly grateful.

He'd also known what he knew now, that it wasn't quite as simple as that. Then, like now, there were things they wouldn't touch on, presumably because they'd wanted it like that. She'd been like a charm for him and he was happier than he'd been in his life before, and knowing any more than he had might have been confusing things needlessly, willing the spell not to hold.

She'd let him know when he first came calling that there were other men who had prior claims to his. Even later, she'd never contrived to conceal that from him. He used to watch them careering down to the farm in their Land-Rovers or catch glimpses of her on a day out in Oxford whistling past in a red Spitfire. He'd been walking past the windows of the Randolph's cocktail bar once and seen her on a stool sipping a long drink with a moustached young man beside her who was biting the cherry off the end of her swizzle stick.

She'd had any number of offers — she told him how many — and in the end she'd chosen *him*. He'd never been able to decide why. Speculating about it even was like analysing his luck, and he gave up. Her father, with his countryman's accidental instinct for shams, had seen through him and detached himself. His degree when the time came couldn't have cut much ice; even Hilary's pride was smothered in indecipherable smiles. It used to console him that her mother was so agreeable: she'd wanted her youngest daughter to grow up cultured and couldn't believe anything else of her, although it was patently clear to the rest of her circle that it was less than the truth. He'd wondered long after, perhaps Mrs Corbett had understood what they couldn't, that the idea of his learning and his social mobility too, both combined, and her daughter's virtues, the practical wisdom of her boarding school — tapestry roses on stale afternoons, long letters to her nephews and nieces to while away the evenings in the fragrant sitting-room — the two somehow, by a natural affinity, belonged together.

Ten years later, with the past still unsolved, he had knowledge enough of them both to know that at least she couldn't become any less to him. She still wore her refinement lightly, reminding him of Astalleigh, breathing it through their rooms like the perfume trails she left behind her on the air. He told people she had the instincts and the little touches he'd never had. He watched her, never tiring of the spectacle; the way she held her knife and fork, the tilt of her wrist when she drank tea, an authority transported by her whole body just crossing a room. Linen napkins in silver rings, walking sticks in the hall, the loo paper cut into single sheets in a bamboo tray.

All that, their intimates were meant to deduce, had been *her* contribution over the years. They could see too he had the sort of pride that meant offering something back in equal measure. It was a talking point among their few choice friends that, even before he was taken on to the company board, he would spend every penny he earned and it was all for Hilary.

They were seeing it, of course, from the outside. A Georgian six-legged sideboard, two Sickert sketches, a cabinet of Venetian glass, in their hall a walnut console table with a marble top. On the other side of the baize-lined front door, if they could have known, things worked themselves out with equal civility and the same tasteful understatement.

Hilary happened to say one day she wished they were able to entertain more people, and the next few weeks were taken up plying the antiques shops till they found an oval Queen Anne table that gatelegged so that they could lay ten places if she wanted. They realized they must have chairs for their guests. They found a set of twelve with shield backs and needle-point seats at a manor house sale and continued bidding till they were theirs. He brought her presents of blue-and-white Chinese bowls and she filled them without his ever needing to say anything (the pot pourri, she announced, came ready-made from a garden centre in High Wycombe). He instigated things which he knew would please her but which would have required too much concentration for her attention if he'd left it to her to decide: in the past couple of years he'd taken out a second mortgage on a cottage clamped to a cliffside near Tintagel, he'd sold her run-about as a surprise and bought her a high-performance Scirocco with an electric sun roof and a rival firm's stereo system. She responded to his concern when he told her that he was happy if she was happy. She mentioned one evening she'd always wanted to paint and the next morning he arranged that an art shop would deliver everything she needed, and when she said she'd like to go on a painter's holiday on her own he told her 'of course' and talked her into taking the most expensive. Her itinerary included Provence and the Italian lakes and they drove up to London together and bought a suitcaseful of lightweight clothes in Liberty's and Simpson's. Of late she had declared abstracts were beginning to appeal to her, and he'd surveyed the drawing-room walls wondering on the possibilities. She informed him there was a gallery in Grafton Street which specialized and he'd phoned up and blanched in the office window when they gave him a sample of their prices.

Needless to say, he couldn't have done it merely on the salary he was paid. He couldn't understand if *she* understood that or if his behaviour from the outset had somehow convinced her that he really could afford it.

His stomach tightened again, there was another wrench as the knife twisted deeper. It was inevitable, he told himself, turning back into the side of the road. He'd begun to suspect they were on to him. It was only a matter of time, anyway. He could think he was like a barometer when it came to people's feelings. He'd already caught the climatic shifts starting among his colleagues, the very slight evasions calculated not to offend, the holdings-back barely perceptible to an uninformed eye.

Five years before, the company, persuaded by his advice on market trends, had inaugurated its research on a new range of 'electronic leisure-ware' for the middle-1980s — videotape recorders one-third the bulk and weight of their originals, a video cassette player that could be slung over a shoulder. He'd studied Japanese developments in advanced microchip technology and the latest simultaneous project was a compendium of video games the size of a slim paperback. The firm was sinking everything it could into his research department, but he'd sometimes wondered if it would ever be enough. Occasionally he would worry about it. Hilary had never expressed any interest in his work and would let any comments he let slip pass her by. He'd immediately regret having said anything, and she'd smile serenely when he apologized as if the offence hadn't even registered.

At some point over the five years, by some accident — he'd forgotten when or how: at a conference perhaps — he'd met someone from one of the American giants. They'd had a profitable discussion — and then another, which considered their shared interests further, and then another one after that. He let them pay for a holiday in New York, which Hilary had loved for its violent, vulgar contrasts to everything she'd been used to. They had another holiday at Christmas time in Palm Beach with one of the executives and his tanned society wife.

It was never directly suggested that he should enter their employ, either officially or unofficially. There'd been some necessary skulduggery late one summer's afternoon in the cocktail bar of the Intercontinental Hotel which had been a little too furtive for his comfort — something to do with an unmarked envelope and the equivalent of four months' salary — but he could convince himself that had only been intended as an expression of trust and appreciation from his American correspondents, and he'd accepted it with the sincerity which seemed owing and with the simple grace he imagined Hilary might have conferred on the occasion.

The two of them began to frequent the Intercontinental on their visits to London. Hilary seemed unthinkingly at home in the muted good taste of their room, watching from the window the elegant life passing on Hamilton Place, never questioning what it meant, how it was they could support this life. He made journeys up he didn't tell her about, meeting his contact (it would be someone different every time) in restaurants in Hampstead or Highgate preselected for them because they were well off the usual business-account circuit. He gave his new associates what experience was instructing him merited a fair price, and he began holding out till he felt he'd got it. He hated the physical act of handing the papers over, the anonymous buff envelopes which his table companions seemed able to slip into their slimline cases with a sort of professional ease, even managing a laugh as they snapped the lock shut. Afterwards, like a penance, he'd stop off at Harrods to buy Hilary something in the parfumerie — an expensive fragrance like Worth or Amazone or Diorissimo, it didn't really matter which: he'd taught her to like them, but he still hadn't learned to tell them apart — and then he'd take the motorway back, winging home in fourth, filling the car with radio voices to kill the thoughts hammering in his head.

Recently he'd caught the news coming through about the Americans and an ambitious new sales programme they were supposed to be launching: attractions included a miniaturized video deck with a compendium of games on recall and a video cassette player lightweight and neat enough to be carried around over a shoulder. He'd been busy the last few weeks assuring everyone it didn't mean anything: 'Stories get about. You know how it is. Talk big, and people are going to believe you.' He would smile encouragingly round the department as he exited early for another consultation with the doctor in Chalfont St Giles.

The four years were beginning to tell on him. He saw it in people's expressions, the concern and caution confused. Faces watched him from the windows as he drove out of the car-park and fixed the white Mercedes like an electric toy on the right track home.

On those rock-bottom days when his stomach was pulling him down as far as he felt it was possible to go, he would try to think of Hilary. Sentimental thoughts. He'd remind himself she was the one constant left, still the woman he'd had such youthfully passionate desires to make his own. He would have the familiar sense too that it wasn't, never had been, quite like that. Facts, his reason would insist, needed to be faced. Facts like having lived their days without each other for ten years and knowing that their evenings after the formal dinner that had been such a novelty once couldn't bring them very much closer again. Himself reading or listening to music while Hilary scribbled letters to girlhood friends or painted noiselessly overheard in her loft. On their weekends dressing elegantly, doing Beaconsfield things, eating out, walking in green gumboots with the dogs through silent woods twenty yards apart.

It wasn't everything. He'd tell himself no, it wasn't everything, but it was enough, and more than most people could expect of their lives. It was the intangible things she was the catalyst for which persuaded him in the end that they lived and loved by a special kind of alchemy that set them apart. The elixir was the aura of graciousness she carried about with her — graciousness, good taste, sensibility, refinement — speaking it in her choice, low-pitched Cheltenham Ladies' College vowels, trailing it through the rooms like her expensive Harrods perfumes he couldn't tell apart. It concerned him very occasionally that he had to lie to her about the lunch trips: it came to matter less and less that what he was dealing in were company secrets, what slightly disturbed him was a double-deal on that which might have been playing on her trust. Might have been — if he hadn't known her better, felt the coldness from her when he mentioned work.

To comfort himself he would try remembering all the things he'd bought to give her virtues a perfect and seemly home. The means had now ceased to interest him. Even the physical discomfort in a way was part of the sacrifice. Driving home he would forget the pain drilling inside: in his head he was surprising Hilary's sculptured dignity as he surprised it every night, catching her mid-sentence on the phone, in the kitchen grandly shaking a lettuce dry, sipping Dubonnet Dry at the window and watching the shadows lengthen in the garden. He lived for the secret link that held the pieces together, locked them into place — Hilary's slow turn-around, the quiet smile, her patience as he touched her lips with his, her approval with him he could feel without hearing it explained in helpless words. It had been the reason why and the justification for it and his reward that made any price seem worth paying.

He had about a hundred yards to go.

A bonfire wafted smoke over a beech hedge. A hired gardener

whirred a Flymo over the Scottish lady's verge. The Tresanton girl had some friends in on the tennis court and he heard their light, trilly laughs.

He'd turned the corner before he saw the car outside the house, a black car, a Golf, tucked up against the verge. He didn't recognize it and made rapid calculations whose and why. He felt detonations in his stomach. He only wanted to be home, safe inside.

He stopped on the other side of the road to give whoever it was a minute or two. He drummed his fingers along the rim of the steering wheel. He was thinking it must be someone for one of their neighbours and was looking at the house for clues when he saw Hilary moving behind the upstairs landing window. His fingers were on the ignition key when he caught another movement and he saw she wasn't alone.

It was hard to tell at first, but he knew it was a man before his eyes could be quite sure.

He couldn't see all of him, the window cut off some of his height. Hilary had her hand on the banister rail and stopped and turned back. The figures for a moment crossed, held still.

His eyes couldn't cope and dropped to the road, the verge, his fingers tightening on the wheel. He could feel the pain drilling deeper, excavating through the lining of his stomach, tempting the unknown. He closed his eyes on it.

He opened them again as the first wave passed and he saw everything exactly the same, the black Golf with the spoiler, the road curving ahead, the cropped verge rising to the beech hedge, the outside of the house. He looked at the house more closely than he'd looked for a very long time. He wanted all the details. He saw the cottagey pretensions he'd forgotten about, the arched oak door and the tiled steps and the rainbarrel and the powder blue shutters and the tiny upstairs windows in the high, steeped roof like eyes watching back, slyly considering.

He lifted the handbrake and let the car gently freewheel past the house towards the corner. Ten minutes, quarter of an hour he'd give them. He'd come back and it would be all over, the car would have gone. He'd sweep into the half-moon of driveway and there would be the crunch of gravel, the chips spinning beneath the wheels. Not the same contained explosion he always listened for, the comforting sounds of journey's end. Something told him there was another journey just about to begin.

He rolled past the other houses on the avenue. His head felt very light and free and apart from all the rest of him. He imagined it tipping itself out, shaking the bits loose.

He slowed down passing the back of the Tresantons' and watched for white movements through the hedge. He lowered the window for some air and listened to the balls being flung over the net on tight racquets. On summer evenings he liked to listen from the garden for the solace of those dependable returns, plung — plung — plung. He came down on the brake, waiting for the end of the rally and then the round of schoolgirl giggles.

At the junction he took the Beaconsfield road. He'd left a reserve in an antiques shop on a Ming countryware bowl. It would put the time off. He'd go back in and say, thank you, no, he didn't think so, it wasn't quite . . . The man who owned the shop would smile at him, shrug his shoulders. 'You're a valued customer, Mr Elverson. It's my pleasure. We'll have something else, I'm sure, before too long. Have a look round, please do, we've some other things.'

He doubted if he could even pretend an interest, just this one particular afternoon of his life. He turned off before he reached the shop and took another side road back up towards the woods. He looked at his watch. He'd try doing a circle.

He concentrated on the red road. He asked the question, but why like this, suddenly so calm? The answer came easily to him, because I've never really known anyway. Realizing the vastness of his ignorance, like a vision of the blackness of space, he understood that confused with the despair there was some comfort too in these things. It had something to do with not thinking too deeply. He had never even considered, so why should he begin now?

He told himself, safe with our secrets.

* * *

He drove the car slowly, slowly.

Other cars passed him, Saabs and Renaults and Metros with their cargoes of capable mothers, children in school blazers and boaters, hockeysticks, empty lunchboxes, docile sad-eyed retrievers. The back panel of a sit-up-and-beg 2CV was covered with ha-ha stickers: '0-60mph in 15 minutes', 'Designed by a computer, built by a robot, driven by a moron', 'Bucks Young Farmers do it in green wellies', 'Italians have more elections than a Chinkie on his honeymoon'. Someone in the back of the car waved to him as it turned off the road at the gate to a farm and bounced on to a dusty, pot-holed dirt track.

He picked up speed a little but dropped back again later, to slower than before, to give a wide berth to a middle-aged couple who were walking one behind the other along the grass verge. The woman in front wore a sensible, quilted navy-blue jacket and a headscarf with a National Trust pattern he recognised over her grey hair; she had a pained, strained expression on her face as she looked away tight-lipped at the rolling fields. The man behind was making an effort to walk upright; he carried a walking stick and his mouth was pursed to whistle. He lifted his eyes at the exact moment the car was passing and nodded towards the windscreen: he nodded cheerfully enough, although his skin was yellowish like someone's whose health has suffered for a long time.

He smiled back at the man from the car, feeling some intuitive sympathy for him. He watched them both in the driving mirror as he followed the road to the next corner: the tweedy husband, head down and suddenly stooped, poking at daisies and dandelions with his stick, the woman in the headscarf and green woollen stockings walking on, setting the pace, and neither of them seeming inclined to speak.

A few hundred yards further on he came to a house that might have been their home. It had leaded windows downstairs and in the steep roof, and chintz curtains and pelmets behind the glass, and a solid oak front door, and there was a rain-barrel just like the one he had to return to. Red virginia creeper and a tangled, gnarled vine of blue wistaria grew up the brickwork. A white froth of Old-Man's-Beard draped itself over the high copper-beech hedge at the front.

For reasons he wasn't able to place for the moment, the sight of such photogenic privacy depressed him. He noticed the name on the plate on one of the gateposts: 'Fairways'. Another sign — hand-lettered on board — hung from the white five-barred gate: 'Private Property. Beware of the Dog'. As he crawled past he heard barking, loud and belly-deep, warning him away.

A few times recently Hilary had spoken of their getting a dog (spoken of it, that is, when she'd felt disposed to speak of anything except her next holiday and galleries of modern art in London she'd read about). A *dog*, for God's sake? He'd wanted to ask her 'What the hell for?' but he hadn't had the courage to do it. Now he realised why she was so keen, because an expensive pedigree Dalmatian or Airedale would be a distraction in the house when there were just the two of them there. And maybe — he pressed the switch to close the window and mute the barking — maybe it would be an added precaution in another respect, the barking would double for her as a warning system, an alarm?

He closed his eyes. A hot searing pain was cutting through his stomach.

Inside his head too he felt there was another heat he couldn't control, a fire that was raging out of control. At this fever pitch he couldn't trust his thoughts any more. It was as if they were making a world for him to confront which had nothing to do with the one he'd always known. Had he really seen what he'd imagined he'd seen? *Had* there been a black car parked on the verge?

The pain passed, rippled away, as if even that might only have been an invention.

He opened his eyes: opened them to a peaceful, still afternoon in this most favoured reach of England's green and pleasant land. Then, driving on, he remembered the couple on their wordless constitutional and the picture wasn't so perfect after all. Perhaps the man had retired early, doctors had recommended it, so he lived now with every new day to fill from waking up to lights out like a terrible yawning hole? Nods and quiet smiles to strangers in their cars: but the private life between him and her, behind the high copper-beech hedge with the strangling convolvulus, that was secret and bitter and to be suffered in silence?

He switched on the radio. A song had just reached its climax. A man's too cheerful voice cut the record short and said it was Barbra Streisand, from 'Yentl', 'No Matter What Happens'. A trailer followed, for a comedy programme called 'Trouble and Strife', about a man who keeps house while his wife works, and a joke about a tin of spaghetti hoops that won't open. The studio audience cackled helplessly, as if marriage couldn't ever be anything else but a hysterical laughing matter.

He turned the radio off. Ahead he saw the triangular island in the road and the fingerpost sign to 'Beaconsfield 3½ miles'. As he approached the knoll of grass the pointing finger looked like something he might have encountered in a dream, the bad dreams he had every time Hilary replaced pudding with the cheese board at dinner.

Tonight — just as usual — they would be having dinner together. He knew Hilary wouldn't allow the routine to be affected. She might be a little behind in her preparations, but she wouldn't attempt to excuse herself. It wasn't her way. She never made allowances for his stomach either, she served whatever she'd decided on — and he didn't dare to object. Tonight would be no different. She would say so-and-so from school had written — Biddy or Prudence or Angela — and tell him what was happening in Richmond or Petersfield or Rustington. They wouldn't discuss the office or his work. She might mention her holiday. Probably he would tell her he'd phone the art gallery in Grafton Street, did she want to go up and see if there was anything she liked? Probably she would smile. 'I'll make a day of it,' she might say, and not invite him to join her: one of her occasional late-home evenings, it would mean, and something Chinese to be picked up from the 'Mandarin Duck' take-away in Beaconsfield.

As she said it and implied the rest, she would be sitting straight-backed in the chair. She would be wearing one of her fragrances. The elegant bottles were set out on display on the dressing-table like an altar in their bedroom, and he didn't know where they all came from, or from whom — with their couturier labels, even more exotic than the ones he chose, 'Halston', 'Chloé', 'Versace', — those perfumes he still couldn't tell one from the other.

He drove once round the open green in genteel Penn, very sedately, to put off another couple of minutes.

It was the *secrets* which they survived on, he was aware: the mystery of Hilary's grace, and of her life before he met her, and of his own past, and of how they spent their days away from each other.

He told himself, safe with them, safe with our secrets.

Pain pricked the lining of his stomach — but only momentarily, then it was gone again.

A few seconds later he remembered the faces at the office windows and the watching eyes. He glanced up at his own face in the driving mirror and performed a look of practised deceit which they would never be able to see through.

In the day's post he had received an invitation to fly out 'with Mrs Elverson' to the States at Christmas-time: not for a house-party at Palm Beach this time but to have the use of another executive's condominium penthouse at Bal Harbour. An instinct told him now it would be wisest, the most cautious move, not to take the offer up. In which case he ought not to mention it to Hilary, he decided, lest she voiced a wish that they *should* go. It was vital, he felt, that they must never appear to disagree on the significant things.

He drove out of Penn, past ideal homes in impeccable gardens. It was like driving through a photograph on a calendar, 'Beautiful Britain', or on to the glossy cover of 'Homes and Gardens', which Hilary bought every month for her magazine pile.

At a bend in the road a black Golf passed him coming the other way, from the direction of Beaconsfield, and he didn't dare to look at who was driving it.

Maybe — or maybe not.

He turned on the radio again. '*Miss* Carly Simon,' the voice chirruped, and he recognised the first bars of the song from journeys to work eight or nine years ago. He even managed to smile, drily, at the coincidence of the choice: if that's what it was.

'We have no secrets, telling each other 'most everything.'

Different strokes . . . . Maybe . . . or maybe not.

He tapped the rim of the wheel and sang along with the voice as he steered for the soft pink dusk ahead of him, descending on the gables and conifers and cultivated lawns of Beaconsfield.

'Sometimes I wish,' the voice lamented and he echoed it, 'often I wish that I never, never, never knew some of those secrets of yours.'

He came to another fork, another hummock of grass and another roadsign. Now, he felt, it was time to go back. A story in a book might have had another ending. But they were left with the rest of their lives to live.

He breathed in, breathed out. In — out. Then he turned the wheel and, after the afternoon's unforeseen delay, he fixed the white Mercedes like an electric toy on the right track home.

Watching Mrs Gordon

She's parading down on the terrace, wearing her lilac swimsuit. She has an audience, of rich old men lounging on sunchairs, who shade their eyes to watch her pass.

She's in her element, anyone can see. Greece has tanned her a deep bronze. She holds out a long thin cigarette — a scrawny man with a ring of white hair on his pate offers her a flame: his gold lighter catches the sun and glints.

I am not young, particularly. I'm not old either — I don't call 'forty-seven' old. I am neither young *nor* old. Let's say I am comfortably 'between'. But perhaps I was past the proper age of falling for her and marrying?

I feel I have to explain these thing to myself. My age. How I was: 'settled': 'set in my ways', I suppose, but not *so* set that she couldn't turn them topsy-turvy.

And now I'm doing what I vowed I wouldn't — I'm blaming *her*, not myself. Watching her fascinated as the old men do while she puts off time down on the terrace. Mrs Gordon. Watching her, fascinated and alarmed.

Or maybe I really *am* too old? Like them, her spectators. In bathroom mirrors in hotels I grow visibly older every holiday: now, each time in the day I look at myself I imagine more grey hairs or another crease on my face.

Sitting in the hot sun doesn't help, but I have privacy out here on our balcony. And from this vantage-point I see everything, of what there is to be seen. I don't doubt she's aware of that too.

She has left them now, her audience, and she's making for the hotel's private beach. In her backless lilac swimsuit cut high at the hips — with her slim, perfectly tanned body that's half the age of mine. She's carrying a bright yellow towel under her arm which I have no excuse for losing sight of — and a book, and tanning cream — and she holds high her lovely head which is full of her own private thoughts she tells no one.

My wife, Mrs Gordon.

* * *

Begin at the beginning.

I knew her parents . . .

Rex Quinn and I worked in the same company, the British arm of an international aviation concern. I'd come down from Edinburgh and risen (with indecent haste, I sometimes felt) to be 'Number Two' in the Home Sales department. Rex was a research scientist — a very able one. We were both in our late twenties, and we got on very well together. Judith, his wife, I liked just as much. I saw a lot of them both at one time. The corner of Wiltshire where we lived turns people in on each other's company, which — in their case — I was glad of.

They were a very 'contented' couple, I'd call them: they seemed made for each other. Like me they had no previous connection with Wiltshire: they'd come from London originally — and gave no evidence of missing the metropolis. Rex was an only child; his parents had been killed in a car accident long before I got to know him. Judith had a father I'd never seen, apparently quite elderly, who lived in the West End and rarely appeared in the sticks where we were: I recognised the 'good address' when Judith told me, in a white Regency square plum in the heart of embassy territory.

I don't know that they meant Diana to be born, Rex and Judith. I suspect they treated sex as an experiment, done for experience's sake rather than pleasure, and for once they'd failed to apply laboratory standards of precaution. They weren't really 'mummy' and 'daddy' kind of people. I don't mean that they weren't affectionate: they were, for each other — and also for their shared enthusiasms in life, which were largely cerebral. And maybe intellect was the problem, having minds that were used to dwelling on other, 'higher' matters than nappies and golliwogs and nursery rhymes. (Eventually they did get round to providing all these things for the baby, but it took a lot of reminding from me. In a sense *they* were the late developers and slow learners, not Diana, who inherited their mental sharpness and used it later for whatever concerned herself.)

A childhood could have been idyllic in that house, a spacious old rectory with a thatched roof, but Rex and Judith thought less than most people do about their comfort; they were very 'take-it-or-leave-it' about their own physical well-being. Their house inside was a celebration of 'mind': overflowing bookshelves, no television set, scratchy string quartets on the mono record player — and the debris of simple day-to-day existence everywhere, abandoned meals and half-made beds and dust. They could blithely forget about food or how freezing a room was if they found a topic they wanted to discuss, or a concert was playing on the radio which they were concentrating on. When she was a baby Diana would often be crying upstairs, in the mullion-windowed nursery where the fluffy toys lining the sill still wore their price tags, and it would have taken Rex or Judith many minutes to realise if I hadn't been there, as I frequently contrived to be on bath nights to lend Judith some help. (God knows what happened when I wasn't there.)

No, they weren't *un*-caring: indeed the opposite was the case, they couldn't ever quite believe the miracle of having given life to a daughter of their own, even if (as I suppose) it was an accident and she'd been the most abstract notion at the date of her conception. It has to be said, though, that's what she always was, their beautiful baby — a kind of scientific adventure for them both, one that had the pair awed and helpless.

*

Diana's grandfather in his salubrious London square took a hand when she was four or five and was proving a little wilful and 'difficult'.

I see now he did it with just cause and for a good end. (Isn't the easing of loneliness a good end? No matter that it was his own loneliness he wanted to ease as well as his grand-daughter's.) Judith's old nanny was requisitioned; a new nursery was furnished; the family rocking-horse was re-painted and had its stuffing replaced.

Diana spent weeks at a time away in London, in the high white town-house in the famous square. Rex and Judith had no objection to the absences, they didn't worry themselves, they knew their daughter was in trusted hands. I was reminded so many times that her grandfather quite 'doted' on her.

'Well, who can blame him?' I said.

Without a trace of self-congratulation they told me they'd called her 'Diana' because she was captivating, like the goddess, her namesake — didn't I think?

'She certainly is,' I replied, and I meant it.

They told me she must be proving it, how enchanting she was, didn't I think that too?

'I'm sure so,' I said, puzzling a little about their need to repeat themselves.

Whenever I went out to visit them they took care to reassure me on the point, as if it also required comfirming in their own minds: Diana was perfectly happy in London. She was quite content, in her grandfather's house. She had absolutely everything she could need there.

* * *

I had to go abroad for several years. By the time I returned to England, Diana was at an expensive prep school her grandfather was paying the fees for. According to Rex (who said it with a quite innocent, guileless smile), Mr Dyson was lavishing all his money on his only grandchild.

When I met Diana again, at the house in Wiltshire which was

officially her 'home', I couldn't help thinking she'd become rather spoilt. I'm not sure what proof I had because I remember that her manners were impeccable. Was it just the cashmere cardigan and the little gold watch on her child's wrist that made me think so? Did I really see or did I just think I could see a pout when her mouth relaxed? Was I wrong in imagining that when she offered her mother her cup and saucer and plate with such a grandly outstretched arm her manner was one of regal expectation? — that *she* would have her tea and slice of fruit cake served first, thank you very much.

She must have been all of nine or ten. She was a beautiful child, but beautiful in a self-conscious way. When she walked it struck me that what she was doing was *parading*, like a schoolgirl in her Sixth Form who courts attention and wants to turn the boys' heads. She smiled at me, but it was a worldly, chilly gesture acted out for her parents' benefit: I was *their* friend, not hers, and I should realise that.

When we would all sit in the garden having tea under a cedar tree, she looked aloof from the three of us. As if she were thinking she was anywhere but here: at her superior school, or with her friends at *their* homes, or at her grandfather's house in Belgravia — shopping with them, dining out, being taken to see shows.

The garden where we had tea had been allowed to go wild. I used to think, was Diana ashamed? — was it that which was responsible for the silences? It's true that her parents had their heads too high-in-the-clouds to think of looking at the ground under their feet — at the uncut grass and the mush of windfalls and the borders infested with weeds. It was a capacious three-quarters-of-an-acre or so, but it can't have been what she was used to when she visited her friends' parents' meticulous country houses and gardens.

She didn't permit herself to become sullen on that account, however: not Diana, her breeding forbade such vulgarly open demonstration of her feelings. But she did something else, equally unsettling: she simply looked through us and past us, with those green eyes which seemed to have a little bulb lit behind them. It was as if we didn't matter to her, we didn't count, or we were like envelopes of air, her head was filled with her own thoughts and she didn't require *us* at all.

Occasionally we went walking together, as a quartet. Judith wore hiking boots and ankle socks, Rex and I put on muddy wellingtons, while Diana accompanied us in polished ox-blood-red riding boots her grandfather had bought her on the Swaine, Adeney and Brigg account he kept for her benefit.

We drove to Avebury a few times and paced circuits of the stones and the grass rings. Rex and Judith read aloud from archaeology books and searched out the ceremonial avenues. Diana was probably bored witless, but endured it all with that regulation smile. Rather ham-fistedly Judith took photographs and sometimes we were both in them, by accident and not design: Diana striding out gracefully in her boots and camel colours, like an actress permanently cued for a shot, and myself unsuspecting, my hands in my trouser pockets, vaguely keeping her in my sights.

We called into tea-shops on the drives home and I thought Diana's face betrayed a certain tenseness as she darted looks at the customers sitting at the other tables. Children of her own age didn't interest her, it was the adults she attended to, and I sat watching those brilliantly green eyes and the Quinn intelligence behind them making the most rapid and discriminating analysis of their social degree and means.

* * *

Also, of course — alas — we are creatures of the times in which we live, and I have to explain that part too.

During the Vietnam period it became public knowledge that the company Rex and I worked for was supplying the U.S. forces with surveillance helicopters and aeronautical tracking equipment specifically developed for field combat. We had a couple of years' very bad publicity in the left-wing press as a result.

Hostility became much more active for a while. It built up quickly: raucous and jeering demonstrations were staged outside the firm's factories and research bases in Europe. Inevitably *we* were included as well in the noisy pantomime. (In Wiltshire we were mainly research and distribution, but in addition there was a small plant specialising in high-precision parts for helicopter navigation systems, and that had to be protected.)

We had no choice but to live with this trouble on our doorstep. It continued for several months. Protesters blockaded us, and police were drafted in from as far west as Bristol. At the height of the business there were half-hearted threats from one of the shipping unions to block our imports and exports. For a while the abuse became more personal. Employees were followed home and excrement and lighted papers dropped through their letter-boxes. After television and newspapers showed photographs of Vietnamese rice-workers burnt with napalm, there was a fire in the main reception area one night: luckily for us, automatic sprinklers coped with it. On another occasion a letter-bomb was half-opened, which scorched a desk-top and singed a secretary's blouse. In the managing director's garden a summer-house was set alight one morning, in the early hours; a few days later, again before dawn, a small incendiary device was hurled through the window of his garage, flaming oil runs on the floor and burning down the timber walls and roof.

It was a worrying, crazy, dangerous time, and sometimes I forget that was the context of our golden age of sunlit afternoon teas, which was really such a short-lived interlude: only one summer and a mild autumn, which turned into an Indian summer, with Judith, Rex, Diana and myself secreted behind the rectory's high walls, in that garden which had been allowed to run wild.

Then, weeks before the news was made official, I learned — I was the first person to be told — that Rex was leaving to take up a senior research post at an American university.

Naturally it came as a shock to me — and took several days of getting over. I would be losing two good friends, after all. I was glad for Rex's career's sake, of course, that his talents were being rewarded. I also wasn't without the pricks of envy: they would be escaping this 'unpleasantness', which showed no signs of abating.

Unusually for Rex and Judith — it was the first time I could recall it happening — they had a plan of operations settled on. They told me at the tea-table one day that they intended selling the house. Diana would finish the next term at her prep school and go to an American one for the following two. They'd decided to send her to a boarding school in New England after that, where she would be only a couple of hundred miles away from them.

I turned to Diana.

'Are you looking forward to that?' I asked her.

She manufactured an instant smile. She had refined those gestures to the point where they took no time at all, she could immediately register on her face whatever you were expecting to see there.

She didn't say anything, in that clipped accent her grandfather's money had bought her. But I presumed the answer must be 'yes'. ('Yes, *thank you*', since she took such pride in her manners.)

'New England's supposed to be lovely in autumn,' I told her.

She put me right. 'Not "autumn", actually. The "fall", *they* talk about.'

How she said the word '*they*' reminded me of the tone the ranters filmed on the television news used for the Capitol administration.

'The "fall", then,' I corrected myself.

'*You're* not going,' she said, reverting to her quiet social-conversation voice which invited you to lean forward to hear. 'So it can't really matter to *you*.'

The smile reappeared on her face, blank and automatic.

'Well, you must write to me, send me a letter,' I hazarded. 'Or a postcard. You can . . . you can tell me what it's like.'

The smile stayed fixed in place, her mesmerically green eyes bored into me, and I knew then that no letter or postcard would ever reach me from Diana in Vermont.

*

The summer and early autumn afternoons in that wild garden became a troubling memory to me for many years — of what would never be again.

In the same month of winter when they were due to leave — it was a dry Christmas without snow, Diana was at home — one night the rectory went up in flames.

I didn't realise as it was happening that it was the rectory. I was sitting watching television in my own house when I heard the fire engine bells and then the ambulance sirens. I got up and walked to the door. I smelt the burning the second I pulled the door open and the cold fell down the garden steps into my hall. Later I heard you could see the blaze from Shaftesbury, a dozen miles away, and after the burning a thick pall of black smoke.

I didn't know, of course, not till the morning. As soon as I found out, from the BBC news, I drove straight over. The voices on the car radio said the protest movement must have been lying low deliberately, to give this latest strike maximum shock-value.

When I reached the house, I saw straightaway the disaster and destruction were total. Even some of the cedars in the garden had taken the flames. The firemen had been doucing the shell of the building all through the night and they carried on for many hours after I'd gone away, shaken and with my inside in knots.

The headline-writer on one national newspaper must have been in high-flown festive spirits when he alluded to the 'Tragedy in Olde Worlde Arcady', above a photograph of the thatched house when it was still a working rectory. The report repeated the details, colouring them a little. The Quinns' daughter had escaped by way of the window in the old nursery at the back and down a drainpipe, surviving a tumble into a rhododendron bush with a gash on one of her legs and assorted cuts and bruises and strains; she was being taken care of by a schoolfriend's parents. The firemen had found her father in his study — but too late, pinned under a smouldering beam. Mrs Quinn had leaped from an upstairs window-sill and crashed into the glass panes of a cucumber frame.

*

For the next few weeks — while no action group claimed responsibility and as the police conducted strenuous enquiries among all the sub-sects and cells of protesters — Judith lay terribly injured in an intensive care unit in a Salisbury hospital. She was in traction and on drips and God knows what else. I visited her as often as I was given permission to, and I was always so upset by what I saw that I was hardly able to stutter out any words of comfort.

The day came in the sixth or seventh week when it was decided that she ought to be told that her husband was dead. For hours after the doctors' ordeal of telling and hers of having to hear she wouldn't stop shaking her head: but she was already starting to lose her will to pull through. Nothing any of us said on that day or on our next few visits could encourage her, we couldn't reach her. Beneath the layers of bandages her resistance was on the ebb; over an intense span of half a dozen days and nights she seemed to be trying to find the desire to live on, but in the end she couldn't.

I believe the quest may even have caused her some amusement. I overheard the nurses saying — with their voices hushed and still uncomprehending — Mrs Quinn had died smiling.

* * *

Seven or eight years later I was in London, walking out of one of the back doors of Harrods, when I heard someone calling her name.

'Diana! Diana Quinn!'

I turned round and caught the perfume of a svelte, sophisticated-looking young woman who marched past me in mink and long suede pencil-heel boots, shaking her long straight blonde hair. I didn't recognise the woman's body — but those penetrating green eyes I did.

The woman who'd called to her spoke quickly, flailing her arms and laughing, then she slung herself into a Mini and shouted goodbye. Diana stood on the kerb, waving after the car.

I never understood afterwards how I had the courage to approach her. I suppose I did it for Rex's and Judith's sakes, for what they'd suffered. (The police had been unable to provide an adequate account of why and exactly how the tragedy had happened: the lack of information and knowledge had disturbed me, even made me feel guilty. Over the years I'd thought of Diana many times and tried to imagine how she was growing up. I also used to ask myself, as if to counter that, how could a career businessman with enough on his mind to worry him possibly be expected to take a jump into such a wholly different experience? I was certainly quite conscious that she occupied my thoughts and that I had a duty to be concerned on her behalf. I'd often reproached myself that I hadn't kept up, that I was betraying the friendship I'd had with her parents. I was curious to know this as well: mightn't she have grown up more like *them* in the interval?)

Now, when I came closer to her, she swung round, she shook her blonde hair and gave me the look of aloof hauteur I remembered from the garden teas. I blinked — blushed too, probably — then I introduced myself. I gave her my name, hearing myself stammering for the first time in years.

'M-Michael Gordon. Do-do you remember?' I asked hesitantly.

With clumsy words I mentioned teas in the garden.

'The garden?' she said.

'That wild garden your p-parents had. D-do you remember?'

She composed her mouth into a social smile, although her eyes were wary and calculating.

'Yes,' she said. 'Yes, I remember.'

I pointed to where my grey Daimler was parked. I explained to her, with more assurance, that I lived in Paris these days. I worked at the company's headquarters, I was only occasionally in London.

Her green eyes thawed. I wonder now if it had something to do with seeing the Daimler and hearing that I lived in smart Neuilly? Or because I found myself asking if she would please have dinner with me that evening? — at the rarefied Connaught Hotel in

Mayfair, which had become my home-from-home in London.

At seven-thirty — as we arranged — I collected her at her grandfather's house. I was invited in and saw for myself how Diana had lived for so long: in surroundings that were stately but, it struck me, also a little shabby.

Mr Dyson was a very polite, very stooped old man wearing a suit of the best quality tweed. He did a great deal of harmless smiling. He didn't look strong — or perhaps it was extreme age that made him seem especially fragile. His grand-daughter performed an elaborate ritual of fussing over him, kissing him, even writing down the Connaught's phone number — 'in case of emergencies', she said, and glanced over his shiny bald head at me. She was smiling too, quite bewitchingly, I thought.

In the car and at the hotel she looked wonderful, stunning. She clung to my arm as we walked in. The *maître* referred to my 'companion'. I couldn't believe it was *me* when I surprised my reflection in the mirrors, sharing a table with this beautiful young woman who seemed to belong inside a glossy magazine. Over coffee — when I'd lit her cigarette with my lizard lighter, which I could hardly hold for trembling — I told her her grandfather was an older man (I also meant 'frailer') than I'd been expecting him to be.

'D-did your mother's death do it?' I asked, leaning forward.

Diana elegantly blew out blue smoke that hid her face and her eyes.

'We don't talk about that,' she said.

She said it not unkindly or ungraciously; she was only letting me know — but quite firmly — that the subject with all its tragic associations had no part in her present life.

* * *

Of course it did, it must have done: I observed that night and on others that followed how close she and her grandfather were, much closer than most people will experience inside that relationship. How, I puzzled, how could those terrible circumstances *not* have decided things for them both and helped to bind them, living together in the same house as they had for so many years?

And yet — what I couldn't understand, when they seemed so necessary to each other — suddenly they were admitting *me* into their home and into their arrangements so easily and so cheerfully. I had the notion that they must have quietly agreed between them that they should. I was forever being invited for lunch or dinner or both when I came over from Paris, which I did as often as I thought I could get away with it. No time was wasted in making me the third side of a triangle. I even stayed at the house now instead of at the Connaught and Diana, anticipating what I had in mind for some future date, quickly welcomed me into her bed. (She proved to be a virgin — and it should shame me to say I was a little surprised by my discovery, given the times we were living in.) Mr Dyson seemed quite unperturbed by our candid glances meant as signals and my contrived exits from the room after her when primitive cave-man lust got the better of me.

Our success socially gave me barely enough time to get my breath back between one occasion and the next. Diana decided which operas and films and plays we were to see; we went together to Henley and Wimbledon and the Hurlingham Ball. Photographs of the two of us began to appear in magazines; she even made *me* look good, for the first time in my life I could remember. The company directors in Paris and their wives took note, and I heard it said they were 'impressed'. We were associated in people's minds and they invited us to their social functions as a couple.

Over those thirteen or fourteen months I was aware that the old man was fading fast, sinking into a decline. It cramped my style in some ways, but I tried not to let Diana see and be affected. Either she didn't notice; or she did an actress's job of pretending not to.

During that time I was becoming afraid for her. I was disturbed to think I was making her dependent on me. She knew dozens upon dozens of people on the party circuit but she seemed to be close to no one except her grandfather and me.

I told myself, surely with her striking looks she could have had any man of her choice? So why *me*? I thought. I also worried about becoming jealous. Yet when I saw her freezing women at parties and then flirting with the other men, I knew — knew intuitively — I was in no danger, flirting was just one of the little social rites her education had taught her.

Paradoxically maybe, I believe now it was a kind of guilt which made me ask Diana to marry me and want to provide for her — guilt that I'd stolen her (from her grandfather principally), that I'd trespassed on her parents' trust because we shared the same bed. (I told myself I was her 'lover', even though I used to wonder if she thought the same way about herself, that she was *my* lover — might there not be an element of ritual in her smiling compliance when we furtively made love in the bedroom next to her grandfather's?)

When I proposed to her, in the Savoy's pink and blue River Room, how readily she replied 'Yes, Michael! Of course, darling!' I was quite taken aback. I remember I fixed my stare on her mouth. I wasn't waiting for a kiss — which didn't come anyway: I was persuading myself (I wasn't sure why) that I didn't really care to see any higher than her mouth.

I couldn't help asking myself again, why me? Why *me*? Was it just because I was the first man who'd ever put the question to her?

I half-admitted to myself at the time that I was too old, the same age her father would have been if he'd lived. Then I started to notice what I'd overlooked, that young men of her own generation, especially if they still had their futures and fortunes to make, didn't appear to interest her. I would watch how those piercing eyes looked through them or past them, how they had with children in Wiltshire tea-shops years ago and with me at those garden teas under the cedar, in the wild garden, on sunlit afternoons.

And eyes are the clue to it.

I have to say that afterwards I didn't care to have our confabulations on serious matters eye-to-eye. That speaks a volume in a sentence, I suppose. When we were married, it seemed to me easier to have our major communications in bed before sleep or on the telephone, or however, any other way than *looking.*

Inside her grandfather's house, until we married, my wife-to-be began to wear purple-tinted sun-glasses, in gilt frames of the helicopter pilot kind. I had contact lenses fitted, which were another excuse for not engaging at crucial moments: I could blink instead and claim blurred vision — and it saved me spying for evasions which I thought must be there in those violently green eyes behind their sensolite glass guards.

* * *

Her grandfather died when we'd been married almost a year. When it happened, it seemed comfortable timing.

It upset her more than she allowed me to see. I'll say that for her. She didn't always conceal her sadness (she forgot about sun-glasses for a while), and I must presume that it was genuine. Some evenings I would come back to our flat in the XVIème arrondissement and find her in one of her dark, despondent silences. The television would be on, or ping-pong electronic music would be playing on the tape-deck, but she was beyond their reach. Or mine.

She urged me to take more holidays, and we did — that part was genuine enough — we went to all manner of exotic-sounding places whenever I could spare the time (and even when I couldn't). I thought it was taking her mind off the business, that was why: I say it in my own defence. Probably it *did* relieve her, but we've never lost that expensive habit — and maybe by now we should. Until then I'd always been cautious with my money (the car apart): after our travels began I became — not reckless or squandering — but, let's call it, 'knowingly extravagant'.

I'm constantly reminding myself. It was done to keep Diana happy; so she wouldn't be dwelling on the old man's death. How can happiness be costed?

But with time she became more withdrawn and enclosed, how I remembered her as a girl before I rediscovered her outside Harrods — and no amount of money I spent could change her back again. I became preoccupied too with thoughts of my own. Was it the travelling that caused it? In bed we lay sleepless on our backs in the heat, with white hotel bedroom ceilings above us like blank white pages to record our thoughts on. I asked myself, over and over, had I married her because I'd felt it was my duty — or to appease my guilt at surviving when Rex and Judith didn't? — or simply because I'd wanted to buy her and own her, like a covetable work of art? — or was it because I'd imagined she needed protecting and that I'd been truly feeling *sorry* for her?

So many questions muddled me. Has the condition of 'being sorry' anything to do with 'love'? Was it 'love' or really '*pride*' at the beginning, having the thrill of a beautiful young woman lying sharing the darkness with me?

* * *

I didn't refer to her parents. I wanted to, I thought they ought to be 'included'. So many of my memories were of Rex and Judith and the house.

I thought too it might help with things between us. But it was made clear to me the only time I mentioned their names that she didn't like me to.

'I'm sorry,' I said.

Pictures flashed into my mind of the tragedy — what I'd seen for myself and what I'd heard, and what I'd read in newspapers about the fruitless police searches to find proof of an orchestrated campaign of violence by the anarchists.

'Of course, Diana. I quite understand.'

She smiled — away from me, so her eyes were hidden: out of the window, down onto the boulevard of plane trees.

A dazzling, utterly empty smile.

* * *

It wasn't till a winter's night in Provence that I began to suspect why she wouldn't speak about them both.

We were in the south for the medieval festivities: so we each made a point of telling the other. But I'd already guessed the truth, that neither of us could face the prospect of seeing in another year in the cavernous apartment in Paris which is still our home — all the electronic sound and vision machines we've bought to distract us aren't so distracting that we can forget our mutual awkwardness for longer than a few minutes at a time.

When we're there we move restlessly around — we're always in motion — in air-conditioned, centrally-heated comfort, in no little splendour. Yet those vast rooms never seem large enough to keep us apart. Not even an interior decorator's tasteful colour-scheme of coral pink and powder blue — 'so restful' — can put us at our ease. We never raise our voices at each other — we never have, not once — but the atmosphere is invariably edgy and tense. I keep remembering the chance encounter outside Harrods — the tea-shops long ago — afternoons in a country garden run to riot and seed . . .

We'd gone driving in the Daimler, up to a village on a hill-top. Turning a dark corner into the square, we saw in front of us a great raging bonfire spitting sparks and, in the glare, a circle of villagers dancing round it.

'Turn back!' she told me. Her hands clutched the dashboard and her eyes shone electrically, like a cat's.

'We'll get out and look?' I suggested. 'While we're — ?'

'No!'

'They w-won't mind us — ,' I began.

'Didn't you hear me?'

She looked desperate, but somehow she was able to keep her voice controlled, to just above a whisper.

'Turn back, Michael! Turn back, I said!' It was a command. '*Please*!'

I did at once, I reversed the car in that fierce orange firelight. Familiar by now with every intonation of her voice and the slightest shifts in her moods, I knew this was panic and her terror was real.

* * *

It came into my head — gradually, a thought formed out of other thoughts. It slowly burrowed its way inside, like a tapeworm. Now it can't get out. It's trapped in there, and never stops wriggling.

She knows, my Mrs Gordon. She *knows*. About that other fire, in the time when the arsonists called the tune and we all lived fearfully — all of us perhaps except Judith and Rex. The crackling thatch — in a couple of minutes the rectory consumed by flames — the prodigal garden burnt and blackened by day-break.

She *knows*. Why it was that *she* escaped and her parents didn't. As if she knew then — ten years ago, when it happened — she would never *have* to go to America, she wouldn't *have* to leave London and miss it, the other girls at school, her doting grandfather who gave her everything she wanted, she only had to ask and (not like her distracted parents) he would hear, the gifts would be given.

Sometimes I seem to see it in her eyes. I can think it, but I can't be sure, not proof-sure. When she's growing bored with me, I see it and I feel it then. When the day becomes slow and heavy at its end, over dinner in a restaurant.

But it's not just in those eyes like green glass, which she makes no effort to shield from me any more. It seems to be there in every single thing she does or else decides not to do.

There are 'rules'.

She doesn't like candles on the table when we go out dining, when we're on holiday or we just have to get away from the flat with its airless, suffocating rooms. She doesn't like bonfires, or even open fires with hearths and grates. She doesn't like naked matches when a waiter lights her cigarette. On even more stressful evenings she's taken to stubbing out her cigarette after four or five nervous draws. When she looks at me she seems to be seeing the truth there in *my* eyes, about her and about me.

Now she doesn't look at me so often, though. She looks *past* me, not *at* me. When I catch her, my Mrs Gordon, she's watching other men, with her Cleopatra eyes ringed by pencil and suddenly large and alert in her face, that face which still opens doors for us.

What's that quote? — E. M. Forster's — the past is a corridor of doors and every one opens into darkness.

Don't trust those eyes, they're like hooks! But the warning is useless, whoever would hear it: it doesn't signify a thing, not when the woman has the huntress's name.

I often wish she would give me some cause to blame her. We would have an excuse for losing control of ourselves then: we could rage at one another and maybe the air would be cleared in the process.

But even if we did, the blame can't be hers. If she were unfaithful a hundred times, it doesn't mean that *I* become any less guilty. What I compound in my imagination only makes it worse, and worse. In that respect, compared with what my sexual jealousy's capable of devising, she's almost an innocent: almost Othello's dream of his Desdemona.

'Almost'. But in that slender gap of definition there exists, just like Othello's, a cold, lightless world of hypothesis — and, so far as I can foresee, no end to it.

It occurs to me that men — all her men, the ones she watches and who don't look away — they *want* to be caught, like me once.

She smiles at them and watches some more. I convince myself that all she has to do then is — calmly, surely — reel them in.

* * *

She's parading down on the terrace, on her way back from the beach.

Her backless lilac swimsuit cut high at the hips is quite dry.

Anyone can see she's in her element. Greece has tanned her a deep bronze. She has an audience, of rich old men lounging on sunchairs, who shade their eyes to watch her as she lingers tantalisingly in front of them.

She holds out a long thin cigarette. There's no shortage of offers to light it.

She draws herself up, stands tall, and blows out blue smoke. She holds high her lovely head, which is full of her own thoughts.

As mine are, those thoughts are walled up inside. The same is true of her as of me: we are never going to admit our guilt by speaking what we think. That would be an injudicious act, it would wreck the game, on this board where we each so subtly gauge our own and the other's moves.

With the semblance of perfect ease my wife flexes her long, evenly tanned legs — and serenely passes on, with those cool, impala strides.

Even when she's walking away from me, I can believe she knows — she *knows* — I'm standing here, out on the balcony, and I'm watching her.

Some couples never find this telepathic closeness after a lifetime together. People who don't know any better call it 'harmony'; they say a man and a woman can be 'made for each other', and they don't see the devil behind it.

Paris

Miss Caldwell was the smarter of the pair. At one time customers would tell her she looked like Rosalind Russell. Even in retirement she had kept her figure (with difficulty) and always wore a turban (in the French style) and good accessories and shoes. 'Shoes are a person's give-away,' she liked to say, speaking from her experience as a fashion buyer in one of the last of the great Glasgow stores in Sauchiehall Street, which had closed its doors at the tail-end of the 'sixties.

Miss McLeod wasn't so meticulous in her appearance, she chose to think she was more 'discreet'. She used to be a teacher in the prep department of a private boys' school in town and for years she'd worn a sexless black gown over her outfits, so variety hadn't mattered. She hadn't dared to change her ways since then and she dressed now as she'd always done, mutely and respectably, because she never knew when she might spot one of her old pupils in the West End, or be spotted by one of them unbeknown. Somehow she felt she owed it to them, not to seem any different from how they must remember her.

* * *

Miss Caldwell and Miss McLeod had met in the late 'sixties, as recently retired ladies and as habituées of Miss Barclay's tearoom in Byres Road. Before their introduction they'd each had a partner to have their coffee with, until at about the same time of one never-to-be-forgotten year they'd been abandoned — Miss Caldwell's fellow-buyer (from Wylie and Lochhead) had inexplicably been wooed by an elderly manufacturer of ball-bearings and married him and gone to live in a nice trim seaside bungalow in Largs; Miss McLeod's friend, who'd been a teacher like her (at the Academy), had returned at sixty-four years old to her calf-country in the windy Mearns — leaving the two Misses, Caldwell and McLeod, seated high-and-dry at adjoining tables and with no one in that roomful of spinsters to speak to.

It was an excellent accident which brought them together, the waitress in starched white linen muddling one's sponge eiffel tower with the other's french fancy. With a gracious wave of her hand and in a throaty voice Miss Caldwell had invited the quietly spoken, bespectacled, beanpole Miss McLeod to join her at her (superior) table in the narrow window wedge of the noisy, high-ceiling'd triangular room. That morning and all the Tuesday and Friday mornings that followed they got on pleasantly enough, just chatting about this and that. It turned out that they hadn't a vast amount in common — Miss Caldwell watched television, Miss McLeod listened to the radio; Miss Caldwell read the *Glasgow Herald*, Miss McLeod the London *Telegraph*. Something else happened to bind them, though. About the third month of the arrangement (they'd learned meanwhile to avoid the topics of television and radio, and referred hardly at all to their different reading) they simultaneously began — consciously, but neither admitting it — to slightly elaborate on what they'd both found they liked to discuss best, themselves.

Miss McLeod 'borrowed' the grandfather of a long-lost friend she'd done her teacher-training with to talk about, a colossal bushy-bearded man who'd been an artist in Paris: that way she felt she could expound with impunity on one of her great interests, Fine Art. Miss Caldwell, who sometimes suspected Miss McLeod dwelled too much on cerebral matters, invented a life which had her working in London in the 1930s, in an up-market store in Regent Street. She hadn't been so lucky, of course, but her stories about 'customers' — Nancy Cunard, Margot Asquith, Lady Mountbatten — sounded quite authentic when she recounted them from gossip she'd picked up from old-hands in the Glasgow store's staff rooms.

'Once Marlene Dietrich came in. Did you know she always travelled with thirty-two pieces of luggage? There was a film on television, on "Saturday Matinee", what was it called? "Shanghai Something" — '

When her memory faltered on a person or a place in her 'past' she was describing, then Miss McLeod (ever on the look-out through the steamy windows of Miss Barclay's for her boys of years ago) took her cue and struck up again about 'her' grandfather's years of exile from Scotland in fin-de-siècle Paris. Every time the city was mentioned Miss Caldwell, resembling one of the mannequins she talked about in her toning fawns and beiges and velvet turbans, would echo the word, 'Ah, *Paris*!', with her own interpretation of what it meant. When it was her turn to speak again she told Miss McLeod, who found it so hard to concentrate on such things and remember them, about the hundreds and thousands of French couturiers' wonders smothered in tissue paper she'd unwrapped from bandboxes in the shops that had been her life. To save the situation, Miss McLeod, awkward in her heather tweeds and oversized cameo brooches and her stout shoes that had a way of pinching her feet however sensible they looked, recited some more odds and ends of information she'd read about Parisian intellectual life in the 1890s.

'I'd love to go!' exclaimed Miss Caldwell in her pan-loaf front-of-shop vowels, 'wouldn't you?' Miss McLeod nodded and replied in her more sedate Kelvinside teaching voice, 'Paris in the springtime! It must be a sight worth seeing!' (Both felt rather sorry for having admitted so candidly in the early days of their friendship that, for all the places they claimed they had visited, they'd never been to lovely, immortal Paris on the Seine.)

* * *

Paris was often discussed, the word 'holiday' would crop up, yet they resisted being drawn into any of the half-dozen travel agents they passed leaving Miss Barclay's after coffee on their two social mornings a week.

They each thought they had their reasons. Miss Caldwell considered that her pension from the store was a little less generous than she might have expected after thirty years of service, and it was hard going keeping herself presentably dressed and stocked up with cosmetics, never mind indulging in foreign adventures. For her part Miss McLeod felt that being seen to be 'careful' with her funds gave her a sort of moral advantage as well as a modicum of mystery, qualities she believed she needed since she so patently lacked her companion's somewhat jaded elegance and style.

By tacit consent Paris remained for them how it had been all along — conveniently in the abstract — and they continued with their stories, retelling them with even more vigour as the months and seasons slipped by. Miss Caldwell talked with glee and much waving of her paste rings about the two elderly sisters who lived on the other side of Atholl Gardens from her, one of whom in middle age had decided on impulse to marry; and after the happy day and the wedding night, had returned the next morning to her sister's flat, suitcases in the taxi, and had never spoken to nor as much as set eyes on her husband in the eighteen years since. Miss McLeod's favourite story sounded more forced and even less likely: she said there was a man of ninety-five living near her in Huntly Gardens, who stayed in his flat alone but set eight places at his dining-table for dinner and ate his solitary evening meal with the members of his long-dead family for company; his windows were lit into the night as he played his wind-up gramophone and walked endless circles round the table and eight empty chairs.

In one sense the two ladies knew they weren't so very different themselves, although they pretended to be with their talk of London and fashion designers who were once well known and that coterie of accomplished painters the critics called the 'Glasgow Boys'. They were both unhappily—if hazily—aware of what was happening to them: that they were becoming afraid of real life and becoming more and more apart from it with the years. They never spoke of their shared fate: it was a truth too awful to encompass properly, encountered so late in the day as this, and neither of them dared to come too close to it, to hazard to that edge. So they held back and didn't speak of it and tried to appear content with the ritual as it had developed: continuing from week to week to week to steer the same wary circle around each other, forfeiting direct questions, working on instincts and imagined knowledge for the sake of harmony, each to preserve her own secrets, the little white lies.

Bizarrely it had taken them both a year and a half just to discover what the other's first name was. At last they'd found out an address too — extracted from countless hints and clues — and several times they'd individually tracked their way under cover of darkness and stood on mushy leaves under dripping trees in a sooty square to spy, but neither had invited the other to her home or could have contemplated it. There was a vague suggestion that Miss Caldwell's flat was filled with Hartnell and Balenciaga creations bought at cost price, and drawers of exotic turbans and gloves, and racks of shoes too good to soil on Glasgow's pot-holed streets; it was never established that on Miss McLeod's walls did *not* hang a gallery of inherited canvases by expensive artists which museums and salerooms would have fought with their claws to get hold of.

* * *

Miss Barclay's tea room closed when the tenement building was scheduled to come down, and they tried other places: a Scandinavian smorgasbord room with dwarf log stools that gave them cramp, the Curler's Arms (nice, with wood fires — but sometimes there'd be a beery smell from the night before), then some of the little healthfood shops that opened up, which served thoughtful food but vile decaffeinated coffee with no taste. Miss McLeod suggested the Grosvenor Hotel on Great Western Road, and Miss Caldwell — anxious about the possible expense with the summer sales coming up — confected a tale she often repeated that season, to do with a man who'd once betrayed her by not showing up for a rendezvous. By way of reply Miss McLeod embellished a story about 'Alistair', who'd actually been her deceased sister's young man years ago, but it was left to Miss Caldwell to presume that *she* had been the object of his affections. 'Yes, I've had my chances all right,' they each told the other wistfully. And talked of Paris again — home of artistic genius and of Chanel's little black suit and that young whizz-kid Saint Laurent — and they agreed how wonderful it must be to live in such a place where romance was the very air you breathed.

Eventually, by mutual agreement, their two shared mornings a week were spent in the upstairs tea-room in the Art Galleries, that awesome edifice with a silhouette like giant red sandstone sugar sifters. Getting there involved a hike across Kelvingrove Park, but the subsidised cost of the coffee meant more to Miss Caldwell than the price of Rayne's shoe leather and although Miss McLeod knew that little parties from her old school regularly paraded the galleries of sculpture and Impressionist masterpieces under the supervision of those pert young wives in polonecks and sling-backs who made teachers nowadays and who'd taken her place, she felt the walk down past the Gothic university with its turrets and steeples and the atmosphere of learning and 'mind' inside the Art Galleries somehow gave her a spiritual authority to compensate for her rather dowdy appearance, which no amount of effort seemed able to rectify.

They would amble round the exhibition rooms after their two coffees and one empire biscuit apiece. Miss Caldwell walked with majestic slowness and the semblance of keen attention — but didn't like to miss a chance to study herself in the glass panels in the frames. Miss McLeod screwed up her eyes behind her spectacles and memorised the artists' names on the plaques for later reference. In the French Room they stopped by the pretty Parisian views — Miss Caldwell (seeing through herself) claimed she liked the 'smudgy' Impressionist ones best, but wasn't able to remember a word of Miss McLeod's painstaking lectures from the times before, about the difference between Manet and Monet for instance. The two of them peered at Paris (Miss Caldwell carefully noting her reflection afloat over the images), they sat down on the benches to reflect, they grew almost tearfully nostalgic for the city neither had visited. (Now they each wished they hadn't confessed as much at the beginning but had left the matter open, as if it might seem they'd happened never to have mentioned the fact . . .)

One fateful day they stayed on for lunch in the Art Galleries and in the afternoon took the bus into town and went to the Glasgow Film Theatre (they preferred to call it by its former name, the 'Cosmo' cinema) and there (with OAP tickets) they settled down to watch *The Umbrellas of Cherbourg*, announced at the doors as part of something called a 'Jacques Demy Retrospective'. Cherbourg wasn't Paris, of course, but they'd come prepared to accept it as a substitute. Not that the closeness or not of the resemblance greatly concerned them when the lights dimmed in the over-heated auditorium. For they discovered with a most unpleasant shock that they weren't educated to suffer the conditions of modern film-watching. They didn't care for this seedy, heavy-breathing mid-afternoon clientele, not one bit. Glasgow wasn't what it was, they agreed in loud whispers. A woman with cropped hair and wearing a black plastic jacket kept watching them and a young couple in the darkness behind groaned grossly like animals. Miss Caldwell was too doubtful to venture into the 'Ladies' even and came out at the end feeling her finery was contaminated with the lives they'd been sitting so close to and also aware of a damp sensation at the tops of her legs; Miss McLeod emerged behind her into the cruel daylight of Sauchiehall Street, trembling like an aspen leaf, her legs scarcely able to support her, sick to the pit of her stomach, quite positive she'd recognised an old pupil at last, sitting in one of the rows in front with his arm wrapped caressingly around another man's shoulders.

* * *

1981's was a savage winter. Snow lay eighteen inches deep in Kelvingrove Park. Miss Caldwell in layers of outdated woollens huddled over a one-bar electric fire in her cavernous first-floor sitting-room. Listening to the radio in her gaunt damp flat, Miss McLeod was almost sure she heard the announcer say the name of her teacher-friend who'd returned to Aberdeenshire when he read out a news item about a woman having been snowed in and dying in a black-out. With this terrible new sadness to bear and no way of confirming it (the newsagent's was at the world's end), she lost much of her own will to live this winter out. Through the icy windows Huntly Gardens was like an arctic wilderness, beyond saving. A pipe had burst in the kitchen, now another split in the bathroom; the gas went funny and wouldn't light, she ran out of matches to try; the radio battery faded to nothing, and she retired without hope to bed, her head humming with memories. She'd exhausted the supplies of food in her larder, was too proud to use her phone to summon help and died of pneumonia and starvation in the course of three long days and nights when the snows blown from Greenland blizzarded across Glasgow's genteel West End and transformed it into a frozenly beautiful winter composition by Sisley or Pissarro.

* * *

To Miss Caldwell's surprise, weeks after the funeral and when the last of the snow had melted away, an envelope embossed with the address of a lawyer's office dropped through her letter-box. She picked it up, turned it over. She braved the cold in the kitchen and made herself a cup of instant coffee — she didn't go out now, she'd forgotten the taste of the real thing — and she postponed opening the envelope till she'd extricated all the excitement she thought she could stand. When she slit the gummed flap with a knife and unfolded the letter inside to read it, she wasn't disappointed by its news. Coming quickly to the point, her correspondent informed her that, after numerous gifts to family cousins, Miss Montague McLeod had stipulated in her will a bequest to be made to her, for a sum of £500.

Two or three days later, when she'd recovered from the shock, Miss Caldwell found her thoughts were turning again and again to an imagined version of Paris, which they'd spoken of so often and so fondly together. She even dreamed of the paintings in the galleries, sleeping slumped over her *Glasgow Herald*. She wondered once or twice if it could be a message from 'beyond'. Quite by chance she saw Perry Como on television singing 'April in Paris'; and the same week a holiday programme did a feature on bargain spring holidays in the city.

One chilly morning with a blue sky she donned a turban (black, out of respect) and a heavy tweed coat (belted and edged with white fur on the cuffs, so very different from the one her late friend used to wear) and walked down busy Byres Road — taking constant note of the state of frost on the slippery pavements — to one of the travel agents. (I do it as my own tribute to a remembered friendship, she persuaded herself.) In the brochures the assistant gave her which she took back home to read, she thought everyone in the illustrations of Paris looked so young. There were hardly any elderly people at all to be seen. It concerned her a little bit that no one in the photographs wore the same sort of clothes as hers or appeared to take the pains about dressing that she did.

Another blue morning with another blue sky overhead she took a brisk walk to a smart little complex of mews shops behind Byres Road, with a purpose already fixed in her mind. It was spring sale time, in one of the boutiques she knew what she would find: a rail of half-price couturier dresses. Inside, positioned at the rail, she only looked at the ones with Paris labels. She found those that were her own size and selected one in festive red jersey wool, with a pleated skirt and a gilt belt and a cowl neck to conceal her least flattering feature. In the mirror, walking like the restaurant mannequins of her working years, she thought they did each other justice, she and the dress. She was conscious of other shoppers interrupting their foraging just to look at her.

She paid for the dress and left the shop carrying it in a splendid silver-coloured plastic bag. On her way home she went into a building society office and opened an account for the £400 left from the lawyer's cheque. It would be a nice little nest egg, she told herself: something put away — plus interest. For a rainy day. For when the bills became even harder to pay. She reflected that sometimes — very occasionally — a little madness was permissible, like the dress: but prudence was safer, in the long run. Nest eggs and rainy days, for when the bills became headaches you went to bed with and woke up with. Such is life, being canny, sensible. If I doubt it, she explained to herself for consolation's sake, think of my friend Monty McLeod, obviously so careful with her money.

Finishing her business in the building society, she noticed the cashier looking at her swanky bag. 'I'm going to a wedding,' she told him, unable to help herself.

She walked back outside through the revolving smoked glass doors, into what was left of the blue frosty morning, disturbed at her untruth. (Her radar set her on the right track home, and she walked automatically.) Even the sun shining now wasn't able to lift her spirits. Her good sense — the red dress and the lie about the wedding excepted — made her feel despondent. When on earth *would* she wear the dress?

Safely past the Grosvenor Hotel and temptation, her legs slowed. Suddenly she felt a panicky fear at the cargo in her bag; she *feared* it, the dress, wrapped like treasure in green tissue paper. (She wanted to smile and shrug her shoulders, she couldn't.) But what she feared even more she realised was still to come, and it was worse than dying in the street could be or hearing a ghost at her shoulder. She envied Monty McLeod her escape, envied her it bitterly. Oblivion couldn't be worse than that ice-box bedroom at the back of the flat and the bleak lightbulb in the fringed shade.

Or maybe — could it have been — she'd intended to help her, her Tuesday and Friday friend whose appalling end had been reported on the front page of the *Herald*, the money gifted to her was supposed to be buying her some comfort?

She continued to walk but slowing her steps still more, to allow the thought to register. It was coming to her, as all important things had a way of doing, out of the blue. She took advantage of the pause to draw her breath and looked down at her silver carrier-bag.

She was remembering something: waking in her armchair one night and hearing the man on the God-slot saying 'It's the mysteries that save us.'

Half-way along Grosvenor Terrace, in the middle of the pot-holed pavement, she stood considering the words. *It's the mysteries that save us.*

Would her friend have known and been able to tell her what the 'mysteries' were? Or could you only discover for yourself?

Did a 'mystery' need to be religious? What about — even — pirouetting for the tarnished oval of mirror in the wardrobe: could that possibly count? Or having a catnap dream in her big comfy armchair? Looking at pretty, 'smudgy' pictures on a gallery wall? Joining in the silly words of a song and hearing Perry Como with a voice like maple syrup say it was called 'the cork-popping Champagne City'?

Harlequinade

She was seeing herself as a bird would have seen her, winging over Paris: a woman walking in a square, shades of grey against white gravel, her hands in her coat pockets.

It wasn't just any square; it wasn't technically a square at all, but the formal gardens of Cardinal Richelieu's stately Palais-Royal. The first leaves had started to fall and she crunched their husks with the toes of her shoes. There was a nip in the air. (They'd left New York in a summer heatwave; deciding to pack her gaberdine overcoat had been a last-minute inspiration.)

The wind was playing pranks with the jet of the fountain and she had to turn her back on the flying spray. At three or four different points on the rim of the circular pool children with mothers braved the wet and pushed out model sailing boats. Dozens of wrought-iron seats were set out on the gravel and she could have had her pick of them, but the day was too chilly to want to sit still.

She made for the colonnades and some relief from the weather. It wasn't much better in there, though, walking from shop to shop. The cold of centuries seemed to seep out of the grimy stone. She looked in the windows, at the Egyptian curios and displays of antiquarian books. She passed a restaurant: net curtains covered half the height of the windows and hid the diners from her, but where they stopped she could see the curved ceiling with its painted cherubs and duck's egg blue sky and pink clouds, stained by time and tobacco. She heard cutlery clattering on to plates and the murmur of voices, and thought how inviting it was.

If the situation had just chanced to be otherwise. . .

She walked away reluctantly, back out into the gravel courtyard.

This time she decided she would defy the cold on one of the seats.

She gathered the folds of her coat, then sat down.

She tipped her cuff back and consulted her watch. It would be another quarter-of-an-hour before her husband arrived. Fifteen minutes to herself . . .

Philip was always punctual. The computer in his head had little alarms for every occasion. That's the way he was. The notes he'd made in the morning would already be neatly marshalled in cardboard folders inside his briefcase, ready for final cataloguing back at the hotel. She would dutifully ask if he'd had a productive morning, burrowing in the records of whichever library he'd been in.

The Russian émigré writers and painters of the twenties and 'thirties were his latest subject of research and he always spoke of them with a passion. Sometimes it struck her that — could it be? — it was becoming an alternative life for him: by writing about it, it was as if he was trying to *be* one of them?

As usual she would adjust her face to make herself appear interested in what he was telling her.

Waiting for him today, though, she couldn't settle.

She got to her feet again. She sank her hands into her overcoat pockets and bent her head to concentrate on the colours of the leaves.

Maybe the exiles in Philip's briefcase had walked here too, it occurred to her, on this very same spot? — she was following in their footsteps? — they'd admired the colours just as she was doing and been moved to their re-creation in words and paint?

She changed direction — it was cold, she grudged those intellectual nomads any more of her attention — and she retreated back into the arcade.

She turned round after less than a minute — heels came

clicking — and she saw Philip fifty yards away in his Nantucket reds and mossy herringbone tweed jacket, his age-less uniform, looking into the bookshop windows with his hand shading his eyes.

He didn't see her till she was almost upon him. He laughed, then kissed her on the cheek.

'Don't tell me, you're waiting for a mysterious stranger?'

She smiled, as seemed to be required, and shook her head.

She thought he looked weary with reading. She told him so. She picked his thinning hair off his brow with her fingers, how she used to push her father's hair back. As she studied him she frowned: his crown would be bald before he was forty — before he was thirty-five.

'Godawful light in that place,' he said. 'Stank of something too — polish. Got what I wanted, though. That's the main thing, isn't it?'

'Of course,' she said. 'If you got what you wanted.'

He took her hand. She knew from his smiles he was glad to see her. But she could never decide how much she herself — the person she was — had to do with any pleasure she appeared to cause. Soon he would seem to forget — he started to be distracted — and she'd feel she became just a pressure on his hand, a presence at his side he didn't need to think about.

He looked into the shop windows and told her about the things he'd discovered. She smiled at the back of his neatly barbered head. She saw past it, to herself reflected in the windows beside him. Definitely not an academic's wife on the outside, she saw to her relief (it showed in the glass): as well as youth to recommend her she had looks, she knew she had, colleagues and neighbours told her so: not the campus wives, but their husbands when they'd loosened up a bit at inter-faculty parties.

Their footsteps rang on the flagstones. Philip was repeating what he'd read in the columns of the émigré daily *Posledniya Novosti*—she was familiar with the name—of August 1932. She wondered if there were people still alive from that time, and—she furrowed her brow—did it matter that a book should be written about them now when most of them must be in eternal oblivion?

Philip's voice was like a rumble in the stone echo-box.

'*Russkiya Zapiski . . .*'

A reflex made her turn her head and look backwards over her shoulder. She wasn't sure why, and she sensed the show of puzzlement crossing her face.

For no reason she could think of she felt her eyes growing in her head.

A low-pitched sough of wind was reverberating the length of the arcade, the way they'd just come. In the middle of it leaves scampered in a circle, sounding like rustling paper.

Why did she continue to look? There was nothing to see. Only a cat arching its back and, twenty or thirty yards away, another man shading his eyes as he peered intently into the window of a foreign-language bookshop.

The circle of leaves scattered; they scratched on the worn stone, then lay still. The wind died, and it might have been her own breathing she was standing listening for.

Her husband slipped her arm through his and piloted her away. She turned herself round to face forward.

She shrugged her shoulders. With her other arm she pulled her coat tighter about her waist.

Ahead of them the sun through the grill-work at the top of the arches was striping the stone with black bars. From a distance — if they could have seen — it performed a curious refraction on them both: splicing them with diagonals of dark so they each seemed to have only half a material presence left.

* * *

The day after the next day — in the Jardin du Luxembourg — she was sitting beneath the shade of trees in the tea-garden, as alive and present as anyone else there.

A dramatic change had occurred in the weather: summer had returned, and even so early in the day the temperature was climbing into the upper 70s.

The tea-garden might have appeared a strange choice of

location. She could have been drinking mid-morning tea in the air-conditioned comfort and soft pink lamplight of her hotel: jasmine tea from eggshell-china cups. But for some reason it must have seemed better to her to be away.

Instead of Louis XVI-style chairs and tables set with crisp white linen cloths there were only folding metal seats and wobbly tin tables, both painted a municipal shade of green; rust showed through and begging sparrows had liberally streaked them with their droppings. But this corner of the Luxembourg had its own charm, which she may or may not have appreciated. From the gravel walks it looked like a dappled sylvan glade. You could have believed Renoir's alfresco revellers must have known the spot and that the artist was going to appear at any moment with a drawing pad and crayons to record the harlequinade of light and shade. Shafts of dusty sunlight sifted down through the trees; the movement of leaves on the canopy of branches at the bottom dispersed it, so the light rippled across the garden as if it were a green forest pool, where fawns might stoop to drink or lovers come to stare entranced at their dim reflections.

Here — open to these considerations or not — she sat on this hot mid-morning: in the sylvan glade, several tin tables away from the 1930s kiosk where people were queuing to buy ice-cream and fizzy drinks. Around her — she turned her head and looked — there were smartly dressed students from the Sorbonne smoking and shouting each other down. A meek, elderly couple out for the day, too poor for coffees, sipped cautiously at the still air. A middle-aged woman with a hawk face and wearing a frilly blouse held a Balzac novel open in her hands and read of events of a hundred and fifty years ago, events which hadn't even happened. Further off, a young couple sat hand-in-hand, as close together as possible, and every so often they pecked each other's cheek.

She watched the pair of lovers for a few seconds, then turned her head away.

Alone at her table she was waiting for Philip to finish his fusty business of the morning. She sat back with her legs crossed and her grey gaberdine coat folded on her lap. Sparrows hopped at her feet and one flew up on to the table and cocked its head at her — but she gave no sign of noticing and looked straight ahead towards the stone balustrades and urns of the formal garden.

A man came close to her at one point; he sat at a table behind her, his newspaper an empty excuse why he craned forward for light. He didn't stay long before he was gone again.

She paid him no attention as he left. Probably his presence had quite failed to register with her, even in the corner of her eye.

This morning there were nearly two hours to fill.

As she looked at her watch, what might she have been thinking? What perspective did she have on her life?

It's the last quarter of the night in the puritan Eastern state where they live.

She pictures the house in darkness, and the other houses where they're known. She imagines her parents sleeping the sleep of the just in their sedate turn-of-the-century villa in professional up-state New York.

In the morning of the next day the flap of their mail-box will rattle and a flimsy air-mail envelope will drop on to the polished wooden floor, on to the colours of stained glass. The news contained inside will be what they expect to hear: that Paris is so interesting, the hotel is central and comfortable, Philip is getting his work done, they've both eaten some exquisite meals.

Nothing she says is likely to excite her parents: they are very placid people, especially now that she gives the impression of having organised her life so ably. They have become well used to these regular mindings from a dutiful daughter and they read them with the same confidence that they used to read her progress reports from school.

Once they'd thought that *she* was going to be the academic. Her teachers had thought the world of her, particularly Philip, who'd been telling everyone great things. In her final year there was a 'hiccup' (the understatement she still used to refer to that time) when her father suffered a heart-attack and, suddenly, she and her mother were called on to have the charge of this heavy, lumbering, cumbersome man in pyjamas and slippers. Even though it was only for a few weeks she couldn't settle to living at home again, with her pale anxious mother seeming to overwhelm her with her requests for pity. Seeing her vulnerability in what should have been her sage years made her panic, as much as the sight of her father did when she watched him teaching himself to move gingerly and unaided about the familiar rooms, wrapped in his dressing-gown and swathed with blankets. The loneliness of those two people in the house after twenty-three years of marriage appalled her.

In her memory they were far and away the most unnerving, dispiriting weeks of her life. She'd never forgotten.

Her father, still weak from his attack, had wanted her to go back to college. All right, yes, she said without needing to think about it and without even consulting her mother, sure, I'll go back. And she did go back, at the first opportunity. She finished the year, assisted by all Philip's patient tutelage after hours. In the background she heard herself called his 'protégée' by staff and students and she knew it was a euphemism for what *they* knew perfectly well the relationship to be. She performed decently if not outstandingly in her end-of-summer-term examinations.

Before there was the obligation to decide what came next, her engagement to Philip was announced. They married a matter of weeks afterwards, at a swift civil ceremony one lunchtime, and she telephoned the news to her mother, who cried with joy and relief. *Match of Minds* the weekly newspaper back home printed above a brief report.

Against the odds, her father recovered in the months that followed. Simultaneously her mother took on a strength she hadn't had before. Philip found himself with the youngest and — he was always telling her — the best-looking wife on the campus. She was left with a husband and a house lined with bookcases, and a mantelpiece of invitations from the other college couples. She also had the private suspicion that she might have acted too quickly, and done the very thing she'd had least cause to do.

Recently she'd taken to watching girls just like the girl she had once been on their journeys to and from the faculty library, and she would have the same thought every time: what a lot of growing-up happens in three years, not physically any more but *inside your head*. When she observed them in their tennis Lacostes and track suits — striding out so nimbly and with a spring in their step, their lithe, tanned exterior charms quite unencumbered by worries for the future — she was conscious by comparison just how much of her own confidence had drained away since her marriage.

Now, three years on, nothing was quite as it had been for her. She wasn't filled with so much awe as before when she saw Philip's name beneath a learned piece of criticism in an academic journal. Even when his book about Proust — *The Skein of Memory* — had been published, she hadn't been able to share all his excitement about the jacket, the type-face on the page, the lay-out, the quality of the illustrations. She'd also become aware during the past eighteen months that her husband was visibly beginning to age: in another two or three years' time they might appear to colleagues and neighbours to be occupying two quite separate time-zones.

Suddenly, in the safety of their puritan East Coast town, she'd started to feel afraid.

The sunlight through the trees patterned a chess-board on the table-top. The bare grass was a harlequin's coat.

She looked round. Her face was pale and anxious for the world to see: how her mother's used to be — and her hand reached up instinctively.

What was her alarm?

For a few moments the tea-garden may have seemed to her to be the haunt of those exiles in the briefcase: hunched men in dark, frayed suits and stiffly-jointed wives in black woollen stockings and queerly-cut costumes, whispering their angry Slavic tongues.

An instinct made her reach forward and grab her bag. She pushed her chair back and sprang to her feet.

She walked off briskly: as fast as she decently could, with scissor-sharp steps.

Putting them behind her — the White Russians and the dispossessed of Middle-Europe — she passed in and out of brilliant sunshine. Her shadow moved ahead of her, falling obliquely over table-tops, empty cups, a newspaper, the sleeve of a jacket — and an unseen hand speeding a pen across a sheet of white paper.

* * *

The third time she appeared she was putting off time in the Place des Vosges.

There she seemed even less aware of her surroundings: as if now she was just letting herself float with the tides.

That afternoon a film team was shooting a man in a black leather suit — a singer? — who was required to amble along one of the gravel paths, touching artfully posed children on their heads.

The director called 'Cut!' after the third re-take. The man in black froze in mid-step; then he went walking off at speed to meet a glamorous woman who'd just pulled up in a white Ferrari. They performed a theatrical embrace and a very public kiss.

The children dispersed, waving to parents, shouting across to them, scuffing their heels on the gravel till the next shot would be called.

Did she notice, anything of what was happening?

Did she realise that the heat had come back to the day, in what was proving to be an Indian summer?

The air shimmered and, consciously or not, she belonged to the coincidence of experiences in that place, at that particular moment out of all time.

Nearby, water sounded tantalisingly from a fountain, dribbling into a shallow stone bowl. Further off, gardeners were spraying the paths with sprinklers to lay the dust.

Leaves slowly spiralled down from the chestnut trees.

The woman walked on the white gravel, beneath the trees, in and out of the sun. She carried her coat over her arm and she was watching her feet. She seemed to be following an invisible line on the ground.

From behind the railings might have made a good point for anyone to watch her. The camera crew and arc-lamps could act as a screen in case she chanced to look up.

She only lifted her eyes when she came to the gates and had to decide where to go next. The Café Ma Bourgogne was diagonally opposite — under the colonnade of arches which runs round the four sides of the square — and her feet turned in that direction.

A white Ferrari roared past. The other traffic cleared, and she hurried across the road.

An elderly man was vacating one of the outside tables on the kerb-edge and she waited for him to leave, then she took his place.

What is there to see and discover about her?

Today it's clear she wants the sun. She unbuttons her shirt cuffs, then her fingers scrape her fair hair back off her face. She nudges herself further back and sits deeper in the chair. She closes her eyes until a waiter comes. (Attractive customers are immediately favourites and never have to sit unattended for long.) The waiter's shadow falls across her, and she looks up and gives him her order.

The coffee arrives promptly, in a jug on a tray. She pours, and tastes. She adds sugar, drinks some more. She appears to be noticing little else of what these moments contain.

Suddenly, following a certain train of thought, she reaches into her shoulder-bag which is hanging from the back of the chair and she takes out a stationer's paper bag; she shakes the thin paper envelope and a postcard flutters on to the table-top.

For the next ten or fifteen minutes her concentration is occupied with the postcard and the business of what to say: what she can allow herself to say.

Occasionally a phrase or a sentence will occur to her and down it goes. Diplomatic words: to her parents, or maybe to a friend from her teen days.

Or perhaps they're not meant for them at all, but for someone else they've never met nor even heard her speak of: for the man who always happens to be there at the same college parties she goes to, whom she's laughingly promised will receive a card from her in Paris?

He has a cottage in Maine, right on the coast, 'away from it all' he's told her. From the skeleton-bones of his descriptions she's imagined it so often in her mind's eye that she feels quite at home there now.

The outside walls are white clapboard. There's a front deck, and an oil-lamp by the door, and from the windows with their cream curtains there's an uninterrupted view across the bay with its shrimping boats. There are some books in the white rooms, but not too many, fewer than in the house she shares with Philip. A wicker basket beside the hearth is heaped with shiny red apples, and carved duck decoys swim on table-tops.

The curtains blow at the windows, bellying over the white floorboards like harmless phantoms. The airy rooms smell of apples and the sweet orchard bark smouldering on the fire and the sprigs of dried lavender pinned to the sanded roof-beams.

Even in the fall the light never completely leaves the sky at night: midnight is smeared with water colour runs, mauve and lemon and green.

She believes it all, what he's told her and what she's filled in for herself—why shouldn't she trust to the alchemy of the two? She's wanted it ever since her lonely childhood in her parents' polished and dust-less villa in the respectable, tidy-verged dormitory town so far inland. She *believes* those fragrant white rooms in Maine: their freedom and grace and the doors always left open, never closed and the keys never turned except to leave.

The sea salt makes a fine grit on the windows, but out of them she sees everything, the blue frothy bay and the long, curving isthmus of land encircling it like a protective arm.

'You'll *have* to see it,' the man's told her in a more intimate tone, while the party chatter swells and ebbs and swells around them and his wife is in another corner of the room and Philip somewhere else, deep in a meaningful conversation with a departmental colleague. 'You'll have to come up and look around. I'll show you. I'd like to show you.'

From the Place des Vosges in Paris she's looking and seeing it.

She sits forward with her elbows propped on the table. She holds her coffee cup cradled in her hands but it's as if it's forgotten for the moment.

From Paris, so far from home — in this silver city of haze, where experiences are as countless as the thistledown seeds which blow up-river in the balmy evenings — she seems to be seeing more than she could have hoped. As the minutes pass the prospect seems to be coming clearer to her, from three thousand miles away.

And Philip?

She knows he doesn't watch American afternoon television with its daily agony of dramas: assignations in French-chic restaurants, hearts-to-hearts in immaculate kitchens, private investigators on one hundred dollars an hour cruising the streets in desirable low-slung roadsters.

He shares a life with Madame Bovary, Odette de Crécy, and Vladimir Nabokov's Russian heroines of memory, and she often wonders if he has the sort of focus-adjustablility that's required to be able to read between the lines.

She tears round the perforations on the stamps; she licks them and sticks them to the card. She takes her pen and underlines the name of the town and the state and the zip code.

She turns the card over and studies the view on the other side. It may be of where she is, the pretty Place des Vosges: the echoing stone arcades and the shuttered rooms upstairs with Paris's ubiquitous chipped pots of geraniums lining balconies: the linden and chestnut trees spelling blue shadows and backwaters of quiet, and the gardens losing more of their greenness the longer you look into the glare of the sun.

She turns the postcard over again, view-side down on the table-top. Her eyes quickly scan what she's written. Her mouth bunches itself, it seems almost to pout — as if she's considering the wisdom or folly of the deed.

But it's done now, the card is a fait accompli.

She pushes her chair back and stands up. She snatches up the card. Is she concerned that her resolution might abandon her, or she might abandon it, before she finds a yellow post-box on a wall?

She inspects the bill and extracts a note and some coins from her purse. She places them on the saucer; she closes the purse and returns it to her bag. She hitches the bag's strap higher on her shoulder.

She deftly moves round the table, to the kerb-side. She waits for a break in the traffic, then crosses with sure strides to the other side.

Now she's under another arcade, which leads away from the square back towards the Marais and the old, high-walled streets with their holy Hebrew names.

In seconds the shadows swallow her — and she's gone.

I come forward when I can find another break in the traffic. I take her seat. I inch it forward, till the sun is on my face.

The waiters are busy elsewhere so I have time to notice the lip-stick stains on the rim of the cup and on the crumpled cigarette tips in the ashtray. The used sachet of matches carries the name and crest of the Hotel Lotti.

It's here, I remember, in the Café Ma Bourgogne that Simenon chose to have Maigret spend so many pipe-smoking, contemplative hours.

Everything has been so neatly discarded: the sachet, the cigarettes and ash, the wrapping on the sugar cubes. The spoon sits precisely in the right hand half of her saucer, the paper napkin is rolled into a ball and placed beside the cup and saucer. The sliding cover on the chrome sugar container has been closed. The paper bag which held the postcard has been torn into half twice and the pieces left tidily in the ashtray, along with the blue edges of the gummed 'Par Avion' labels.

The waiters walk past and don't realise that the occupancy of the table has changed, and my sex; they register only a shape, and the absence of irritation. Even the couples at the tables on either side seem unaware, and each pair talks to one another of what concerns them most, across the tops of their cups and between cigarette draws.

I creak back in the rattan chair. From here, mid-way under an arch, the view towards the garden is uninterrupted.

The fountain dribbles into the stone basin, which is sculpted like a giant clam shell. The hot gassy air dances along the gravel paths. On the corner of the square a man and woman kiss: they seem to be sucking out each other's soul.

The sun re-emerges from behind a high, wispy cloud. The canework on the empty chair opposite me chequers lozenges of light and shade on the flagstones.

Sunlight washes across the table and over the evidence she's left behind, that at a certain moment on a certain day she found herself here. Hot light spreads across the snow-glare white of the waiting page, and the hand on the wrist at the end of the arm, and the moving pen.

Palladian

'Rand. Mrs Rand. But the name won't mean anything to him.'

It was a bad line, considering they were only speaking across Rome. The man at the other end sounded impatient with her. She didn't know why. Was is because she didn't speak Italian?

'He's very busy, signora.'

'Yes, I'm sure. I'm sure he is. I appreciate that.'

'Prego?'

'I said — ' She shook the telephone receiver. 'Two-thirty, did you say?'

'Two-thirty.'

'That will be fine. Thank you. If you could please let Mr Kendall know — '

'What?'

'Two-thirty is fine. Thank you. Grazie.'

She replaced the receiver. In the mirror her face was flushed. The Rome midsummer sun had already striped it bright lobster pink. I look a sight, she thought. And what on earth have I let myself in for now?

*   *   *

She ran a bath, added salts, and lay soaking in the restoring warmth for half an hour. She turned on the radio and let the excitable gabble between the records wash over her, like the scented water.

She got out, dried herself, and put on her bathrobe. In the

bedroom she piled up her hair, then sat down at the dressing-table to make herself up.

She did a more thorough job of it than usual. She attended to the fretwork of tiny lines like cracks at the corners of her eyes and her mouth. She widened the area of blue on her eyelids: silvery blue to complement the grey of her eyes.

She noticed how the lipstick was starting to shake between her fingers. Concentrate, she told herself, *concentrate* — and then felt she was only making her nervousness worse.

She decided on the pink silk dress. The next minute she changed her mind: she would wear the mauve one. She put it on. Yes, she thought: mauve looks less — less 'insistent' than pink. It 'befits' a woman in her middle-fifties.

She found the mauve shoes. Then she chose a navy blue pair instead. Matching dress and shoes would look just too studied.

She picked up the book from the bedside table. It opened at the page where the girl's first appearance was described: fair hair, brown sunned limbs, restless hands 'flexing long fingers', an 'anxious' mouth, grey eyes 'misted with doubt'. How clever of a man to notice things like that. But of course that's what makes a certain sort of man become a writer, his 'apart-ness', his distance and detachment.

She thought of Donald. How much do husbands notice? They notice price-labels and calculate if a purchase is worth the outlay — is it a good investment?

Donald was acquainted with Howard Kendall's book, he'd even read it once, or made an attempt to.

'Sorry, Joanna. Not for me,' he'd said in his deliberate way. 'Not my kind of thing at all.'

He'd told her what he didn't like about it, rhyming off a long list of faults. To her it wasn't any more than you might have expected from a mind trained to the blind discipline of accountancy.

'Another thing, what's the point of looking back? *I* can't, not in *my* work.'

'No, Donald.'

'Where would I be if I did that?'

She'd looked dutifully blank.

'Tell me too, why's it called *Other People*?'

'Because — ' She'd floundered. 'Because — '

She'd watched him turn to the last page to find out how the story finished.

'What happens?' he'd asked her. 'Does he marry her?'

'Oh, no. The ending's left open.'

'Don't see the point of that, do you? Either he gets his girl or he doesn't.'

'I don't think you understand, Donald.'

'I don't think I do.'

He hadn't understood, not one little bit. The 'sympathy' wasn't there, so how could he have seen what the point of the book surely was? — that to the adult man telling the story, stories don't just 'end': the girl, Julia, lived in his memory and remained for all time his constant *ideal*.

* * *

In truth the book's last page had always left *her* rather confused too — and, in ways she couldn't explain to herself, discontented.

What Donald had quite failed to recognise was that *she* was the girl. Too many of the details matched to make the resemblance coincidental: Julia's physical appearance, the house where she grew up, her parents, her experiences at school. It had shocked her reading the novel when it came out, after she'd recognised with a jolt the author's name and photograph in the newspapers.

Concerning Howard Kendall, she still wasn't able to comprehend — how could someone have concealed his feelings so well as he must have done at the time?

The book jacket said the prose was 'ardent' and 'poetic', the author 'makes an elegiac myth of the girl who lived in the faded Palladian house in the park'. But in reality he'd hardly known her. Or so she'd always thought.

Millicent Spencer, the vicar's daughter, had vaguely introduced them to each other at a church bazaar her mother had declared 'open', when they were twelve or thirteen. They'd exchanged a few words in the refreshment tent. He'd told her he had just won a 'free' scholarship to the cathedral school in Wells (he repeated it, he'd won a '*free*' scholarship). She remembered becoming bogged down in a tongue-tied description of her new boarding school in Worcestershire, and her mother calling for her before she managed to finish.

The next year they'd picked apples together once, after she'd found him in the orchard. After that she'd chanced to meet him one Sunday near Christmas, skating on Fox Hole Field pond. The next spring or summer he'd followed her one afternoon when she was walking into the village to post letters. At some later date he'd had the message passed to her by bush telegraph that he was curious to see inside her home, and she'd obligingly found an occasion for him to come when she knew her parents were going to be in London for the day and she would be left alone with Mrs Hunter: she'd shown him the rooms they lived in and she'd enjoyed answering all his questions, even the ones about their dull daily routine out of term-time when there were only her parents and herself and Mrs Hunter and Mrs Hunter's husband and, sometimes, a schoolfriend to fill the house. Much later, when she'd finished boarding-school and he'd gone to university, they'd danced one waltz and one quickstep together at Millicent Spencer's coming-of-age party. That was the sum of it.

Parts of the novel she didn't like: the descriptions of her parents, who hadn't been as handless as he made them out to be — the passage about the hunt meeting at the house and then the riding-out, which was unnecessarily cruel and sensational — and, possibly worst, the idea that there was some unhappiness living inside Julia despite her blessings in life, a dissatisfaction which the character couldn't find words for. But in essence it was her and it could be no one else: it was *her* past — described so faithfully she could only marvel.

She felt that the likeness to her was better than any photograph's could possibly be because the image *moved.* However often she read the book, it retained its capacity to surprise: in the same way the character of the girl finally lacked predictability.

Life's like that, she knew: it has an *elusive* quality. That gave the book its 'truth', although people like Donald and the critics in newspapers sneered at it because it didn't match up to their requirements of a novel.

She didn't doubt that at the time Howard Kendall was perfectly bright enough and sure enough of himself to know what he wanted to do in the book. He certainly couldn't be caring *now* what his reviewers thought. He was successful, the hardbacks and paperbacks of his novels were forever reprinting; he lived in some splendour in Rome; he told magazine reporters he would spend six months researching a new idea and another nine months writing it up through its different drafts; he was a 'General Knowledge' question on radio quiz shows.

Today, after all these years, she'd called his telephone number. (She'd been very surprised to find it in the directory; fate seemed to be ordering her this opportunity.) She'd spoken to the taciturn secretary; an appointment had been fixed for two-thirty, when Mr Kendall would be able to see her.

'Briefly, signora.'

'Yes. Yes, of course.'

In middle age they were going to meet again, and now at last she would have her curiosity satisfied.

* * *

She paced the hotel room, its length and breadth, maybe two dozen times.

She thought it best to eat, so she phoned room service and ordered a chicken sandwich and fresh fruit and a glass of orange juice. While she waited she sat and watched some lunchtime television. She kept looking at her watch. She re-varnished her nails. She stood up in case she was creasing her pleats.

When it came, she could only nibble at the lunch on her tray. After she'd eaten what she could she picked up the book and glanced through it again. A few times — no, more often than that — she'd tried to supply her own ending to the girl's story. What she envisaged hadn't anything to do with Donald. It hadn't even to do with Howard Kendall, photogenic social celebrity, who'd acquired his good looks quite mysteriously in the course of a school year when she was away at Malvern. The conclusion she always imagined to her story was a very simple one: *she had her freedom restored to her*. She won it back, the marriage knot was untied, and suddenly she was able to think and choose all over again what she might do with her life. Beyond her new conclusion, though . . . well, she could never imagine quite *that* far, she hadn't been born with other people's powers of creativity.

Sometimes — when she was feeling very clear-headed — she thought your ambition should simply be to live with as few disappointments in your life as you can possibily manage. But whenever she read the tender, lushly nostalgic book through in full to its smudged ending, she wondered if there needed to be any disappointments at all.

She debated whether to leave a note for Donald. He was lunching at the Hassler with the directors of a Swiss-Italian electronics company. She decided 'no', she wouldn't. She was trying to prove to him she could take the change of life gracefully and she knew how her visit would appear to him, silly and sentimental and demeaning herself.

Taking a last look in the mirror she thought she looked creditable, with her face camouflaged. The Roman sunlight wasn't so damning after all.

* * *

A taxi drove her the few miles from the Hilton into the city. It was a slow journey in crawling traffic, and the delay and the prospect of what was to come began to unnerve her.

The driver deposited her outside a high flaking façade in a noisy side-street in the centre. She didn't take time to look up at the building but fished notes out of her bag to pay the driver then immediately rang the bell on the green metal gate before her resolve had a chance to evaporate completely.

The man's voice she'd spoken to earlier called out of the

entryphone. A master control was pressed and the door in the gate swung back.

She was met inside, at the top of several flights of marble stairs. She could feel her strength sapping from her after the climb. The secretary, as he introduced himself, proved to be a slender, handsome young man in a neat charcoal suit. She found his fashion-magazine good looks oddly discomposing. For a moment she was back at Millicent Spencer's twenty-first birthday party, catching her breath as Howard Kendall walked into the room, the free-scholarship boy turned into the darkly suave sophisticate, like an artist's line-drawing of brooding, sculpted virility in a men's-wear's advertisement.

The secretary's handshake was brief but left her fingers aching.

'Will you wait?' he asked her, pointing the way ahead into the hall. 'Please?'

'Of course,' she said, sounding winded. 'Yes, of course.'

He closed the double-doors behind them. He opened another door with a baize lining on the inside. After a couple of minutes she could hear voices, two men's voices talking in Italian. They seemed to be bickering.

Luckily for her she wasn't standing too near when the door flew open. She watched the secretary as he strode out, with his anger darkening his face.

'He's coming,' he said curtly and walked past her, into another room, a bedroom. He slammed the door shut. (He must live here, she thought.)

When Howard Kendall made his entrance she had no proper expectations to compare him with. She hadn't seen him for more than half her life. His air of youthfulness surprised her, though, considering they were exactly of an age: his trimness, his hair still black and receding only very slowly, the elegance of his walk, his good looks preserved. His navy blazer and white pleated trousers had a stylish continental cut. He smelt, not of tobacco like Donald, but of an expensively under-stated eau-de-cologne.

He didn't shake hands but indicated where they should go.

'Mrs Rowan?' he said, leading her into a high cool salon awash with daylight.

She blinked her eyes.

'Rand, actually. Rand. It was a terribly bad line — '

'I'm pleased to meet you, Mrs Rand,' he said quickly in a quite class-less voice she didn't remember. 'My time's a bit limited. I'm afraid it's not always possible to receive callers.'

'No — '

She recognised the sourish smell when he spoke, which the eau-de-cologne couldn't conceal. Donald's breath smelt the same after his expense-account business lunches. He walked quite easily, however; his balance wasn't affected as Donald's was sometimes.

'You used to live in Somerset, Mrs Rand? Didn't you say?'

'Yes. Yes, I did. Once. Do you go — '

'No, I haven't been there for years. I expect I'd feel like a ghost now. I don't think I shall be back.'

'Well, of course not,' she felt obliged to say. 'It's a long time ago, isn't it?'

There was a momentary enquiry in his eyes. Or so she thought. Then he smiled, showing all his teeth. She smelt the wine again.

'It's — It's very good of you — ,' she began.

'Please sit down, Mrs Rand,' he said.

She lowered herself on to a black leather sofa. The room was a bewildering mixture of furniture styles, antique and up-to-the-minute. All very expensive and put together with some thought, she judged.

'This is a *wonderful* villa,' she said. She was feeling nervous and slightly sick but she tried to sound enthusiastic, putting as much brightness into her voice as she could.

'Palazzo, actually,' he corrected her.

'*Palazzo*, I'm sorry.'

'One of Palladio's, no less.'

'I used — '

I used to live in one, she was going to say, in a Palladian house. In the backwaters of Somerset. Not genuine Palladian, of course.

'In the style of'. Very run-down. But it was so complicated to explain. Later, when he realised who she was, she would say to him. He would remember.

'Did you know,' he said, leaning back in his chair and stretching out his legs, ' "Palladian" also means — I made myself memorise it once — "Of or pertaining to Pallas, goddess of wisdom. Hence, pertaining to knowledge". Oxford English Dictionary. Aren't you impressed? Tell me you're not — I dare you.'

He grimaced with his mouth. (She'd noticed how the corners naturally pulled down; she'd just been thinking what a tribute to his appearance it was that nothing was taken away as a result.)

'I'm — '

'I'm always telling people what it means,' he said. 'But they never seem very interested, for some reason.'

'Oh. But it *is* interesting. I'm sure it is.'

'Really?' He raised his eyebrows quizzically. 'Anyway — ' He pulled himself up in the chair and crossed his legs. 'The house is one of the perks of my job, you could say.'

'It's — ' She crossed *her* legs too, as becomingly as she could. 'It's quite a perk to have. With *any* job.'

'A "proper" job, you mean?' he asked her, his sharp author's eyes not seeming to register her legs.

'Oh, I didn't mean that. Not at all.'

He smiled again. She saw the smile was to put her at her ease — he'd only been teasing her. (Was not noticing her legs also to put her at her ease?)

'It's a marvellous job to have,' she said. 'What you do. I really do think so.'

She didn't know how she could presume to talk of his 'job'. He was reputed to gross a considerable income from his chic novels and magazine stories about the 'beau monde' and their fashionable neuroses. When she'd known him it was in another life, in the sticks of Somerset, which didn't seem to have anything to do with this luxurious, sunny siesta existence above the streets of Rome.

She realised he wasn't going to let the subject of his writing go.

'I write froth, Mrs Rand. *Froth*. The flotsam-and-jetsam-brooklet-of-consciousness, let us call it.'

The words had a prepared ring to her ear, he'd spoken them before, on other occasions like this one, to his other callers.

'I'm sandwiched — I *nestle* — between adverts for sanitary towels. Now, *that*'s the reality of people's lives, is it not?'

She didn't know what to say, to agree or to disagree. She was also more than a little shocked.

'Well,' he qualified what he'd said, 'not the reality of *my* life!'

He laughed.

'I don't know about Tomasso, though!'

He laughed again. The secretary had reappeared. He stood at the door, fastening the ventless jacket of his suit: he grinned in response. A rather mechanical and humourless grin, she thought.

She cleared her throat.

'You — I think you underestimate yourself,' she ventured. 'As a writer.'

'Sweet of you to say so, I'm sure.'

'I do enjoy your books.'

'So, you're a fan, are you, Mrs Rand?'

'Well, yes. I suppose so.'

'Have you any doubts on the matter?'

'No. No, not at all.'

'Jolly good. Well, then. That's got that subject over with. Something to drink?'

'I — '

'Something wet, Tomasso please.'

The secretary walked across to a sideboard and poured three ready-made pink concoctions from a glass jug. His strong fingers undid the top of a bottle and bubbling soda water fizzed into the tumblers.

'Ice, signora?' he asked her in an automaton voice.

'Ice? Oh, yes. Yes, please.'

'Tomasso doesn't need to ask *me*, you'll notice, Mrs Rand. He knows what *I* like.'

A look of concern appeared on the secretary's lean face as he turned his eyes on her. She preferred not to see and swivelled her head away.

'He's used to me, you see, Mrs Rand. How I operate. Good old Tomasso.'

She accepted the drink gratefully. It was a distraction. Clearly she'd come at the wrong moment, she'd interrupted a domestic tiff.

She heard her loud swallows. Some drops spilled on to her mauve silk. She laid her hand on top of the damp mark.

'So, which is your favourite?'

'My favourite?'

'Story.'

'Oh. Story. Of course — '

She watched how careful a check he was keeping on Tomasso's movements about the room.

'Well — '

'I've written so *many* wonderful books,' he said. 'Have I not?'

She didn't understand the tone of his voice. She tilted her head to one side, a gesture that meant 'please explain'.

'So many gems,' he continued. 'How *could* you decide? How can you measure such paragons of literary excellence — nay, genius — against each other? It's impossible, isn't it?'

She smiled. Then she sensed that smiling wasn't the required response.

He closed his eyes. He was shutting them out, her and Tomasso.

'Well, it's *my* jolly old nest, Mrs Rand. And I'll foul it if I feel like fouling it.'

She didn't know what he was talking about. Nests and fouling them, in this free-and-easy language he spoke. In one of the room's mirrors she saw how aghast she looked.

Outside the traffic of Rome squealed and horns blared, she wondered how she was only hearing the din now.

Suddenly, without any warning, the secretary clattered his tumbler on to the silver tray on the sideboard. He turned on his heels, and went marching out into the hall.

They both sat watching his departure. His shoes echoed behind him as he disappeared downstairs. He sounded as if he must be sprinting down the staircase.

After the glass doors on the ground floor had rattled shut there was a long painful silence in the apartment.

Down on the street the traffic thundered — like sea over rocks, the comparison came to her.

She didn't know if it was her place to speak first.

'Heigh-ho, Mrs Rand,' she heard him say at last. 'Looks like just you and me left.'

She stretched her mouth to a difficult smile.

'Yes. Yes, it does, doesn't it?'

She put her glass to her lips and swallowed.

'I'm always asked . . . ' He paused. 'What is it I'm asked?'

She continued to smile. She realised he was speaking to cover over the silence, to help disguise her embarrassment. Her smile felt as if it was sticking on her gums.

'Oh, yes,' he said. 'I remember. "Why do I write about women"? '

She cleared her throat again. 'Yes,' she repeated him. 'Why do you write about women?'

'Funny you should ask that, Mrs Rand. I should say — ' He closed his eyes; it seemed to be a habit with him. 'What is it I say? Because they're more interesting. Because they have depths. They suffer. They're victims.'

She nodded. 'How can — how can you understand all that, though?' She craned forwards a little as she asked her question. She wanted to appear interested, but she was also concerned to hear his answer.

'No trouble.' He fluttered his fingers. 'I hardly think about it, I should say.' He held up his glass. He wasn't going to tell her any more. 'Still thirsty?'

She shook her head, disappointed.

'You'll excuse me if I indulge?' he asked, getting to his feet.

'Do — please.'

'As you see, we're self-service now.'

She watched his stylish amble across the room to the sideboard. 'But no one's indispensible,' she thought she heard him say or something like it. He took hold of the glass jug and from a height expertly tipped the contents into the tumbler in his other hand. He tasted, tasted again, then added a measure of a green liqueur. He shook the pink and green together.

'Cheers!' he said, still with his back turned to her. 'Your very good health, Mrs Rand! The very best of jolly rude health!'

* * *

That day he came to the house she'd served them both barley water. What did he remember now of their afternoon? She had almost total recall of it, perhaps because her life had had less excitement and fewer events to make an impression than people might have presumed.

She hadn't forgotten her return visit either. A verbal invitation arrived, via Millicent Spencer, that she should visit *his* home. She'd told her mother, who seemed uncertain but didn't say 'no'.

It turned out to be the oddest day. The chauffeur delivered her in the old Daimler. She was embarrassed to discover when she got there that his parents were both out as hers had been. While the car and driver waited outside in the road, they sat in the cramped lounge among glass animals and antimacassars drinking ersatz hot chocolate. Then he gave her a conducted tour of *his* house, using words and expressions she'd used to him the time before—'ye gods', 'jolly' this, 'bally' that—and pretending to her that this wasn't what she knew it was, a semi-detached in an ordinary suburban-looking road tagged on to the back of the village by a jerry-builder, but an edifice as grand and distinguished as her own rather dilapidated home had been in its glory days. Every so often he laughed and shook his head at what he was telling her in his dead-pan delivery, speaking in a put-on wireless announcer's voice.

His methods confused her. She lost her bearings, in the end she wasn't certain where she was, in a real house or in his imaginary one. She didn't know what she should be making of *him*, her guide who wasn't.

She tried to show herself interested, which only made him exaggerate more. In his parents' bedroom he opened the drawer in the dressing-table and showed her his mother's make-up. 'My mother doesn't use cosmetics,' she said, then wished she hadn't.

Without asking permission he started applying it to her face, sounding very knowledgeable about the business and seeming quite unembarrassed by the physical contact. Just as unpredictably, she simply sat on the spindly stool and smiled at the transformation that was taking place in the scratchy mirror and let it happen. It happened as easily as things happen in good dreams: it was like a spell he'd put on her, it was as if his purpose was to turn her into someone else, another person, not herself.

*   *   *

'I think you do it very well,' she told him. 'Writing about women. *Very* well.'

He raised his glass as he eased himself into his gilt bergère chair. He bowed his head. He closed his eyes and sipped. He seemed to be far away in his thoughts.

She didn't know what else she could say.

There was another long silence.

She took advantage of it and his closed eyes to watch him. Then she recognised a familiar face in the pier-glass behind him, and she studied herself, or the image of herself.

What she saw wasn't encouraging. Her host was surviving middle age in far better shape than she was. Perhaps the mirrors at the Hilton were purpose-made to flatter? Here she looked putty-faced, and decidedly squat. The pier-glass let her see what she didn't like to acknowledge, that she was spreading to fat in places. The aerosol colouring she used for her hair showed up as lurid brassy yellow, not gold. She'd always known that the long fair hair of her girlhood hadn't improved her appearance with the years, so she regularly 'toned' it — but she hadn't noticed the defects of the operation so glaringly before. Seen in this light she looked exactly how she dreaded to imagine herself: the rather jaded, sedentary, over-fleshed fifty-six year old wife of (what could beat it for dullness?) the 'Group Finance Director' of an international storage and material handling corporation.

The rings sparkled too brightly on her fingers, she realised. Her mother would have disapproved if she'd been alive to see. Donald loved big stones and glitter, though, that was his way. Just as he'd loved the general notion of her background without really knowing the first thing about it. Even when he'd seen how she lived in the big house, in dusty, threadbare rooms with radiators like coiled serpents which never worked, he'd described it to other people differently: now when he told his business colleagues in senior management, it became *Brideshead Revisited* and champagne brunches and lingering sunsets over the cupola. He'd fallen in love with the idea of her: and she'd married *him* because, 'trade' or not, he'd been the first person to ask her and because she'd sometimes had the scary feeling (without the remotest justification, she could now see) that she would never be able to escape from those rooms — in her disturbed later adolescence she had the same warning in the same recurring nightmare in bed, that unless she grew her hair like Rapunzel her complexion would fade to the paleness of the bleached panelling and she would be fated to live the rest of her life like one of the woven figures trapped in the moth-nibbled tapestry on the dining-room wall.

A stupid panic, of course. But real enough then.

She replaced the glass on a tray on the table behind the sofa, noticing the fine tapestry deer-chase on the wall at the back where the full strength of the sun's rays didn't reach to discolour.

'You must — you must observe women a lot,' she risked saying. 'To understand them. To make sense of them.'

'No. Not especially.'

He shook his head and she shook hers. How did he do it, then?

'You — you write out of *sympathy* for them?' she suggested.

'I'm not conscious of that.' He shook his head again. 'You take it all — well, out of yourself.'

'Oh, I see,' she said. She didn't think she did see.

'Always you're just writing it for yourself. *About* yourself. Sides of yourself.'

She uncrossed her legs. She couldn't really make sense of that remark.

'In my modest opinion,' he said, 'writers are the bloodiest, most selfish breed of life on this earth.'

She tilted her head to one side.

'Barring secretaries, that is,' he told her, and let out a long, world-weary sigh.

'Secretaries?' she repeated him.

She was going to tilt her head again, to the other side. It was a ritual she often performed with Donald, it meant either 'I don't really believe you' or 'I cannot understand you'. But just then her host leaned across to the table with his outstretched fingers; they found what they wanted, a sheaf of papers. He reached into the inside pocket of his blazer for a pen, a fountain-pen. He lifted his eyebrows as he unscrewed the top, and held the nib up to the light.

It took her a few seconds to realise what the actions all meant.

'Oh. Excuse me,' she said. 'You're — you're busy?'

She picked up her bag. She eased herself out of the squeaky leather sofa and felt her neck firing. She turned away from the pier-glass, decorated with what looked like white stucco mermaids or sea-sirens. She was wishing now she'd tried harder with her appearance over the years, much harder.

She stopped at one of the windows and looked out.

'It's a splendid view you have,' she said, delaying, needing to summon up courage to explain the purpose of her visit. Or *was* there a purpose after all these years?

He came and stood beside her. She might have been looking out over the park at home that day of his visit to the house: she'd felt sadly ashamed as he stood at her shoulder and for the first time she'd become aware of how untidily high the grass was, the sorry state of the driveway, the paint flaking from the window frames.

'What a lot of mirrors,' he'd said to her, in his soft Somerset burr which the school in Wells was already starting to iron out.

'I hadn't noticed,' she'd told him.

'I thought that's what they're for.'

'What they're for?'

'To notice yourself in.'

She'd stood pursing her lips unsurely. At fourteen or fifteen he'd had the makings of his adult good looks but his face had also been capable of taking on such strange, indecipherable expressions.

'Do you have a yacht?' he'd asked her.

'A yacht?' She'd laughed. 'Of course not, silly.'

She'd thought that day he was going to kiss her. She'd felt his hot breath on the back of her neck. She'd wondered, why not? Then, when he didn't, she'd turned round and seen a look flash across his face: like pity, and a kind of pride combined with it, triumphing there in his foxy-keen scholarship boy's eyes. He'd lifted his eyebrows. She'd been confused. Don't look at me like that, she'd wanted to say.

She caught the fragrance of eau-de-cologne. She turned round.

He wasn't looking at her this time. His eyes, which had always seemed to her too alert for comfort, were trained on the street. A crinkly vein throbbed in his temple.

She followed his gaze. Down on the street the secretary stood talking to another tanned young man in a white convertible. They were both laughing.

The driver had a woollen jumper tied round his shoulders, a bright emerald colour to draw your eyes. One bronzed arm was draped along the back of the vacant passenger seat, the other hand combed back through his fair hair.

The secretary was talking exaggeratedly, as if he were impersonating someone. The young man in the open sports car was being hugely entertained; every time he laughed he dropped his foot down on the accelerator and revved the engine.

'I think I should go now,' she said.

Her host said nothing.

'I — ' She coughed a dry frog out of her throat. 'Don't . . . don't you recogn-'

Her voice trailed away. She noticed the vein standing up like a little flex on his temple. She saw that his hands were clenched and his knuckles were white.

'My husband,' she said. 'I have to meet my husband.'

The word seemed to prompt him out of his reverie.

'Your husband?'

'I'm in Rome with my husband.'

'Don't let me keep you, then,' he said.

'No. Well . . .'

'I don't care to think I stand in the way of other people's pleasures,' he told her, with a solemn, drained face.

They walked to the door, and out into the hall.

'Have you forgotten something?' he asked.

'Have I?'

'You look as if you're trying to remember,' he said. 'Where you left it. Did you bring anything with you?'

'No. No, I didn't bring anything.'

She had, of course. And I'm leaving empty-handed, she thought. (It occurred to her as an afterthought when they'd reached the double-doors, maybe 'empty' isn't the word, if I compare my lot with others'.)

Out on the landing her heels clattered on the marble. They sounded vulgar and screechy. *His* shoes were silent; almost furtive, she thought, as if they were meant for stealing up and down flights of marble stairs in palazzos notorious for ancient shenanigans.

'I shall leave you now,' he said. 'I must get back to my work. Thank you so much for coming.' His voice was perfectly insincere. He smiled, a multi-purpose smile for callers.

When his face relaxed, the smile faded and she saw the full extent of the tiredness and strain revealing itself.

She was remembering articles she'd read in newspapers — and, clearer in her memory, a programme on televison she'd watched, about pairs of men or women who lived together, beneath a shared roof. She remembered how *subtlety* had seemed the one quality missing in lives that photographed so well and seemed so lucky. Underneath was tension, guilt, suspicion and lack of trust, and a terrible lack of forgiveness, as if by not excusing a partner's weakness you made yourself stronger and less vulnerable.

'Can I ask you to please see yourself out? The door into the street should be open.'

'I — I'm very grateful.'

'You haven't brought a book to sign?'

She shook her head. 'I'm — I'm sorry. How thoughtless. *Should* I — ?'

He took a small notepad from his pocket, scribbled his signature on it with the fountain-pen, and tore out the page.

'Shall I dedicate it?' he asked. 'For you? What is your first name?'

'Joanna,' she was going to say. Then she gave him, not her own name, but that of the character in the book.

'Julia.'

For a single second she thought she caught a possibility collect itself behind his eyes, behind the furrows on his brow. Then he looked down, to attend to the pen flowing across the page, dashing off the words in florid, extrovert script.

He presented her with the piece of paper and performed a little mock-bow from the waist. She thanked him; she folded the paper without looking at it.

'Thank you,' she repeated. 'Very much.'

'I hope you both enjoy the rest of your stay. You and your husband.'

'Yes. Yes, I'm sure we will.'

He held out his hand. She accepted it hesitantly. It felt unnaturally cold, on this very hot day.

Hers when she took it back felt clammy. She watched him standing flexing his. He looked as if her female heat disgusted him.

She believed she began, very dimly, to understand at last: how all the pieces — so shaken up before — fitted together to make a not very pretty picture.

* * *

In the enormous gilt mirror she approached as she walked downstairs — Palladio's stairs — she saw the flush on her face. He was standing watching her from the landing, like an owner on the deck of his yacht or a captain on the bridge of his ship, dressed in his expensively tailored white and navy leisure wear.

A woman on the turn, he must have been thinking. The look on his face told her he was pitying her.

All she wanted now was to be back at the hotel, with Donald, packing for their flight back to London. The cosy car journey by headlights through leafy Berkshire lanes to home. Safe inside, shut the door. Close the curtains, switch on the lamps in the warren of low rooms. Back to their quiet, steady, anchored lives with no surprises allowed.

Her heels dragged on Palladio's marble in her speed to get away. She felt circles of dampness under her arms.

She didn't look back, she didn't dare to.

Slowing very slightly on the flight beneath to draw breath, she thought, maybe he's recollecting this moment — to use again? For another novel? And by a sleight of memory it won't be 'Julia' he uses, but another name that came into his head one summer's afternoon. (Beneath her she was conscious of her legs starting to run again, spiriting her away.)

'Joanna'. 'Joanna Someone'. He'll have forgotten the details of how it happened, and who the woman was exactly and what she looked like: only that it was the same day, the terrible day of the beginning of the end, when Tomasso went sprinting down into the street to meet a laughing boy in an open white coupé who wore an emerald jumper knotted on his shoulders.

Other

When he'd pushed through the crowd, elbowing himself forward to the bar, he saw the man wasn't there. He didn't really need to look, a sixth sense told him that there was no one among all those present whose life had any bearing on his own.

He was relieved, and disappointed too.

The barman leaned across the counter and he ordered — he couldn't think what — a sherry, he said. Amontillado please, he added, picking the safest. The 'please' sounded unnecessary but pubs confused him, they weren't his usual way.

It was too hot for a start, too many people, and too much noise. Men in business suits like his own jostled and heaved; they drank and they laughed, and some of them lounged against the frosted windows.

Now and then as he sipped he could make out various women's voices. He glanced covertly at the couples who had assignations with each other, couples in rut, who couldn't keep themselves apart.

He stood and sighed into his schooner of rather tepid sherry. He looked round again several times, but there was no one in the mahogany room he recognised, in the scrum of bodies.

He heard the din of laughter and voices washing everywhere, it was like the waves of the sea, and he let it just lap over him.

He lifted his glass, drank a mouthful from it, and swallowed.

Again he sighed. Even the shock of recognition would have been better than this: this hesitation, this scrupulous care, this impeccable restraint in every single thing he did.

*   *   *

He'd always seen him in different places.

He'd seen him blurrily in a white Kensington square at dusk, and illuminated by an Embankment sunset, and standing hailing a taxi in the lights outside Wheeler's Oyster Bar. But he wasn't only a ghost of the twilight hours. He'd sighted him on a busy bus one morning and in a tube-train at the half-past-five rush hour. He'd glimpsed him once drinking coffee at the white marble counter in Fortnum's Mezzanine room, perched on a stool between two shoppers draped in fur coats. Another time he'd noticed him in Pall Mall, with bright sunlight behind him so that he seemed to be steering a path through cathedral shafts of London's dust.

He aged every time, of course. But that's how it should be, he'd realised: just as *he* wasn't the same man on every occasion it happened. If spirits didn't also grow old and suffer the same end as ourselves, the streets would be cluttered with generations of them: druids trying to negotiate swing-doors, Tudor ladies trying to lift the weight of their dresses through tube-station turnstyles. Spirits, he was convinced, they passed on whenever those they knew died: the candle was snuffed out, and its shadow disappeared in the same instant.

It was curiously consoling to him — he wasn't sure why — that the face and shape had adjusted with the years. He couldn't have given anyone a very adequate description of the face or the outline, even if he'd been brave enough to want to confide: neither could he close his eyes and visualise the features in any degree of exactness to himself, to his inner eye. He just *knew* when it happened: seeing the bodily gestures he was both familiar with and not familiar with, which might have been his own but weren't.

He'd never gone near enough to identify the features, even to learn the colour of his eyes: yet indubitably it *was* him, the man who seemed to be his double.

It was from observing the man that he'd come to understand

this, which he believed to be a general axiom: namely, that you can be intimate with a person — a wife, say, or a husband — and at the same time be apart from them, you can seem to share in the same things they do but simultaneously be perfectly detached. In the opposite sense, that's what it was like with this other person he mentioned to no one: he felt he'd known him and known him well, all his life, even though the two of them existed as strangers to each other.

It would have been so difficult, so *bizarre* to explain . . .

All he could do was follow an instinct and ensure that their eyes never engaged — and that they never came close enough for him to discover if there would be two shadows mapped on the ground, or just one.

He still hadn't heard the man whom he imagined looked so like himself either speaking or laughing, or as much as clearing his throat. But he realised it's impossible to hear in London anyway. When are the streets done with their roaring traffic? Even in Kensington backwaters or in the private cobbled yards of St James's the traffic and the roar are there, although they're muffled like the sea. Perhaps yards away car brakes squeal or a taxi meter rattles, enough to remind you that you are never quite alone. Alone with the silence of other people's being — or your own.

* * *

He didn't come across him when he was with Elaine. He couldn't remember having seen him from the windows of any of the flats they'd lived in. Years ago he'd thought he spotted him on the Heath one evening, approaching dangerously close to the house they were in then: but it happened in archaic gaslight, on the track beaten in the grass like a pilgrims' way, and as the man quickly walked away he couldn't be certain.

He knew that he wasn't married, the other man. There was a discreet fussiness about his appearance which he didn't associate with the condition of being a husband. He would be dressed in neat, good-quality tweed suits cut to flatter his frame, and polished expensive-looking brogues, and a hat — the broad-rimmed kind it took courage to wear — which was tipped eccentrically off the straight. Probably, to judge from his exterior, he didn't have a city job. Something artier, he preferred to think: he sold pictures for a living or he advised on them, or he wrote reviews for antiquarian magazines — or perhaps what he wrote wasn't criticism but fiction, situations and characters that evolved out of his imagination?

He spent most of the journey between work and home searching him out in the faces of other men: those crowded round the Red Lion in Duke Street and spilling out of its doors on to the pavement, beer-glasses in hand, or those who surged along Piccadilly in droves while he stood waiting for a bus, or those he watched from the bus windows as it careered bumpily along the Brompton Road. Occasionally he would find someone was staring back at him and he hadn't realised: a man much younger than the one he was looking for — a student with books, or a dapper shop assistant pulling at clean cuffs, or maybe a muscular labourer, with shirt buttons undone and his chest showing.

He would see them staring back at him. Sometimes they looked blank: or they might seem uneasy, or indignant, or sly. The difficulty for him was to look away quickly enough, and not to be caught firing, which he would feel himself doing without fail, getting hot and sticky and troubled under the collar.

* * *

With Elaine there, it never happened. Other people presumed . . .

But wasn't it the case, he'd thought many times, that what *they* 'saw' was only what their preconceptions told them they were 'seeing'? When his friends from the office and from his university days had come to the wedding at the little church out at Kew, on the Green, they'd received the images they'd expected to receive. And afterwards too, at the reception in Elaine's parents' garden, with everything so dainty and ship-shape, a blue-and-white striped marquee, baskets of flowers, a string trio playing 'This is my lovely day'. A late marriage, they must have been telling each other: late better than never at all, though. Derek and Elaine.

On the drive to the airport, settling awkwardly with Elaine in the back of the taxi, he'd suddenly for the first time seen the man who could have been himself. He'd come walking out of the Gardens, between the gateposts. It happened just then, at that same moment on their wedding-day when they were being driven past. He couldn't clearly distinguish the man's face, he wore a hat and the late afternoon sun sinking behind the Pagoda was throwing confusing shadows.

That spring day was when they had truly begun, in earnest, the visitations. Before then he'd seen men he would have liked to resemble, but he hadn't ever caught such a close physical similarity to himself in anyone — the general outer appearance of himself at least: the manner of walking with the knees stiffly jointed and raised high, the upward angle of the head, the body's vague list to starboard.

Even Elaine noticed the manifestation, the likeness between them, and seemed startled. Till, as the taxi swept by, he laid his hand on her arm and she relaxed, or pretended to relax, and whatever doubt had crossed her mind remained inside her, her secret.

They didn't speak about what they'd seen, then or during the two over-long weeks of the honeymoon, and the man sporting the felt hat who'd come walking so casually and so opportunely out of Kew Gardens hadn't been mentioned again in the eleven years since.

* * *

He stood uncomfortably at the bar between pushing shoulders on either side of him. He fingered his schooner of sherry. The straining shoulders under the shades of grey flannel felt weighted with muscles.

He observed the delicacy of his own hands.

It was always his custom to go straight home from work. Recently the pattern had been disrupted. Elaine's mother was ill and she'd been going over to Kew to visit her. She'd told him she would be later back tonight, eight o'clock-ish.

'Have a drink somewhere, Derek, why don't you? Enjoy yourself!'

So, he reflected, what was happening to him now, this was caused by fate? By fate, and not by himself?

Sherry had a habit of going to his head, and he wondered if he'd been wise. ('Wise' — an Elaine word.) He still had the walk to Piccadilly ahead of him, and then the journey home.

When he looked up into the mirror he saw he was being watched. The watcher was a man, young, in his twenties: not the regular sort of customer, his skin was streaked with dry plaster or paint, probably he'd come off the building site in Jermyn Street. He wore a red checked shirt, unbuttoned to reveal a glorious Roman-eagle of hair like furze on his chest.

He lowered his eyes seconds too late to the schooner of sherry. Out the corner of his eye he was aware of the man, like a blot of red, moving out of his range of vision.

He lifted the glass up, tipped his head back how drinkers in films did, and swallowed.

For a while he felt its sweetness swilling around in his head, behind his eyes, into his neck.

He watched his fingers on top of the counter. Long and bony, like a bachelor's. He shifted on to one leg and stood watching the fingers as they played with the stem of the glass.

Elaine had been going off to visit her mother on two or three afternoons a week for the past four or five weeks. She would return home by quarter-past-seven, saying very little, her face rather flushed. Her mother had caught flu after Christmas and certainly she *had* been rather poorly, but Mrs Coutts came from robust, resilient, independent-minded stock. Other husbands, it struck him now for the first time, they might have had cause to be concerned about events. To be jealous — or, even, suspicious. He didn't really know what feelings he had about it, if he had any at all. Elaine's absences inconvenienced him maybe: but this was only what it had been like before he married, when he'd had the tiny sun-trap flat behind leafy grey-brick Great Ormond Street.

He raised the glass, meaning to drink from it, but put it down again. Remembering . . .

Then all his time had been his own. He would saunter home through Bloomsbury after work, past the university where he'd been a student. He would linger of an evening in late-opening second-hand bookshops. After a makeshift supper he would take himself off to the British Museum Reading Room and scribble half-heartedly at poems and stories which never seemed to get completed: more — he liked to think — from lack of proper application than because he'd lacked talent.

And somehow since then the years had slipped by. Eleven years, going on twelve. Instead of the cramped attic rooms above the tailor's in Lamb's Conduit Street there was now a first-floor flat with high ceilings in a very respectable, tree-lined crescent in South Kensington, and Elaine with her casseroles and yoga and batik-printing, and Elaine's favourite George Shearing or Duke Ellington to listen to after dinner while he read the newspapers or an occasional novel and she thumbed through magazines with glossy liberated-looking women on their covers — who, oddly, discomfited him.

Nowadays they had their routine, the two of them, and he could feel that this life of theirs was very safe, and very predictable. Sometimes it would occur to him too that — as they both passed into the middle part of middle age — the routine was starting to become just a little bit dull.

And yet, he was also prone to thinking, was he seeing only part of the picture? — seeing what it was he'd persuaded himself he could 'see'? An instinct would nag at him some evenings, that truth may be other than we choose to perceive it, more is hidden from us than we are ever capable of uncovering . . .

Turning the stem of the glass he wondered how he would react if he chanced to catch a glimpse of Elaine on his way home. Say, travelling through the evening traffic in a sports car with another man. A younger, better-looking man.

It wasn't beyond the bounds of possibility, he suspected. He'd learned on their honeymoon that Elaine's expectations of a marriage — in the simplest physical terms — were not his. He'd often puzzled how she could have discovered the things she knew about what she called 'emotional fulfilment' ('sex', she meant), sounding like an article in one of her modern women's magazines she read with the shiny covers held too high for him to see past.

* * *

The shoulders on either side of him pulled apart.

'Having another?' a voice seemed to be asking at his ear, but sounding far away.

As it spoke he was thinking who else he might catch sight of on his way home. Every five or six weeks their paths fleetingly crossed. His — and those of the man he might have been. His other self. The one he'd left behind in Lamb's Conduit Street, in the sunny, constantly airless flat above the tailor's, and who'd come walking out of Kew Gardens wearing a hat (from Lock's perhaps?), with the Pagoda and fading sunlight behind him casting shadows. The one who'd persevered, and who wrote for a living, and afforded good clothes, and frequented art galleries in the middle of an afternoon, and perhaps was visiting the London Library or Spink's or a portico'd club whenever he happened to spot him in St James's — remembering caution as he did so, standing back to observe him and always keeping that vital distance between them.

'Or maybe you want to have something else?'

The voice didn't fit with the face half-concealed under the hat, or with the body — a little trimmer than his own — inside the well-cut tweed suit.

'You'll have to pay for it, though. Ten quid, let's say.'

The voice he was hearing belonged to the streets, but not to these gracious, prosperous ones with their coloured and distinguished history.

'I don't suppose it's going to be your place. So, what about mine?'

He lifted his eyes and saw it was himself he was looking at in the mirror behind the bar, among the bottles and glasses: his own face pale and pinched, his business suit creased and the knot of his tie askew.

Automatically he freed his elbows and straightened the tie, how Elaine always commanded him to.

'Okay, lover boy?' the voice whispered. 'Prettied yourself up?'

He had no idea where he was being led when they'd left the pub. Past Wheeler's, and past the open-fronted fishmonger's he would have glanced into at any other time, with its staring, jelly-eyed wares on the white slabs and, even on warm days like this one, the sensation of cold from the gurgling runnels of water, as if nature intended to momentarily disturb in the very heart of a city.

He was following the checks on the red shirt. Sinews pulled in the man's bare arms with their fleece of matted gold hair and plaster streaks, and he longed to give himself to this different kind of commanding strength.

He watched a knot of muscles twitching above one elbow. He heard Elaine's voice reminding him that gentlemen never *never* roll their shirt sleeves beyond the elbow.

He wasn't paying attention to the passages and alleyways they passed through, their names, which was which. He hadn't realised St James's had so many of them. For thirteen years of walking past he hadn't realised.

As they crossed a dusty courtyard — he was thinking in those seconds of furtive Venice, where the honeymoon of the two mature newly-weds had ended — he failed to see there was another man standing in the shadows made by the peeling walls. As they crossed over, out of the sunshine, the man in the red lumberjack shirt solemnly nodded a signal over his shoulder to the other one who waited.

He failed to see that gesture too. His sixth sense had abandoned him. If he'd noticed, the nod might have warned him; he might still have had the ghost of a chance to get away.

He did hear faintly the heels of other shoes, a third pair, an echo on the flagstones behind them. But the sounds of London are as vast and engulfing as the sea, and all else drowns beneath it, in that rolling and infinitely repeating swell.

Thicker than Water

Elspeth

Twenty, thirty times a day, bustling round the flat, she reminds me of the good sense of the 'arrangement' — and so of her own charity.

She tells me it must have been God's doing. God realised at some point that the flat was too big and too comfortable for one person's needs, God wished that there should be a 'reconciliation'.

God wished . . .

I'm trying not to listen as Florence busies about the sitting-room, puffing up the cushions. In the sitting-room of *her* flat.

I watch her in the window while she works. For the moment I'm just her suffering sister, sitting stooped over the *Telegraph* and running tired eyes along the lines of print.

She looks at me and I lower my eyes. Now she's congratulating herself on the lectern, which was her idea: slats of wood the building's Happy Harry banged together for her, which can straddle the two arms of the wing chair.

She rubs at a mark on the sill.

'It's clearing, Elspeth. That's good. You'll be able to get out after all, I expect. Helen said about two.'

I spot another advertisement among the little boxes, among all the contraptions illustrated that help to make other people's lives go round: the pocket computers I can't make head nor tail of and the quartz digital wrist-watches and the minuscule cassette players you wear strapped to your waist and listen to through earphones. I smooth the page flat and find the box again with my finger. 'Get-U-There. The Tried and Proven Electric Caddy Chair for Sportsmen, Gardeners and Invalids. The British World-Beater. Satisfied Customers in Five Continents.' I read the text with great care. The possibility of escape cheers me always during these bright and breezy morning sessions as Florence sweeps about the room making so ridiculously light of her seventy-nine years, flicking her duster with the sure, easy aim of the supple-jointed.

It's the evenings which gall me most, though, so that I have to sit writing letters, to Matty and Jean in Havant and Shropshire, to pretend they're not happening.

The evenings even more than the interminable afternoons and our genteel walks about the expensively landscaped gardens. And the embarrassed conversations in sheltered nooks with our neighbours, which never take us further than the time before. And, later, the unconscious hours before dinner in my bedroom.

At dinner we keep up the old formalities. Helen from the town comes in and knocks herself up in the kitchen, so that Florence can serve on the Worcester and pour stilled tap water into the blue Venetian glass and allow herself the luxury of her reminiscences.

I have my own reminiscences while she talks and talks and never listens.

We're both at one of Ma's and Pa's dinner parties: we're trying not to see Uncle Julian, who's winking at us and tucking his hands between his thighs: at the other end of the table we're trying not to see Mrs Kidd in her black lace shawl, who's closed her eyes and is beginning to nod her head over the soup bowl.

And then between the nods, it's after the War. Florence is twenty-one, it's her Big Day: and I'm nineteen, and we're listening to Mr Holliday's band from Honiton pumping out jigs in the marquee in the garden, making everything seem right again. We're thinking in the quieter moments of Pa and Geoffrey and the others — the two sets of cousins and the Suffolk Bury Huttons' — and at the same time we're trying not to think about them: they're inside us, a part of us, as they'll always be (so we keep telling ourselves).

But then when the band strikes up it's the here and now of Peter's flesh and blood we abandon ourselves to. Peter — with what Mama, quite won over to him now, proudly calls his 'military bearing'. He's smiling at someone's joke. Mama is Obviously Keen. She raises her eyebrows at Florence behind his back. He looks more handsome tonight than I have ever seen him, much fairer in the creamy light of the paper lanterns that swing on tipsy wires above our heads: our father's colouring perhaps, when he was young. Mama, studying him, looks radiant. Florence merely looks glad, and relieved, easing her hand beneath his arm as they stroll to the front of the tent.

Then it happens — quite unexpectedly the wind gets up, it's blowing in through the flap. The lights splutter. Our shadows flare up the walls, disporting themselves across the angles of the canvas ceiling. Something then or now tells me this is a moment of truth, fate intercepted at some crucial split second, and I can't for the life of me, then or now, understand how I can know that. Time stutters. The shadows criss-cross in wild, illogical combinations.

After that the candles recover their equipoise again, the shadows finish scrambling up the canvas and disappear, all is as it was: Florence smiles, arm-in-arm with Peter she passes me. We find something else to look at other than each other. There's a suspicion of hesitation and that's all. And an unwinding in the air and a funny waxworks smell after they're gone.

Why, suddenly — now — am I living it again? For three quarters of my life I've been learning to forget, because I told myself I needed to. Convincing myself almost that I had. What's this awful racking vengeance that comes with the wisdom part of age, so merciless it won't even let me be when I shut my eyes at night and pray to Florence's God to please give me sleep?

*

After lunch Florence commandeered the lectern, to arrange all the photographs in strict piles. The flats, she explained rather tartly, aren't made for those of a nostalgic disposition.

The process of elimination became slower and slower, though. She stopped several times and passed across a photograph, asking me how much I remembered. Not waiting for my answer.

'The party, do you remember? And the band? What were they called?'

I saw her face shining, in spite of herself.

'The three of us, just look! Happy as Larry! Not a care! We were so young. Younger than you think when you close your eyes and try to remember.'

Sentimental smiles — then she felt for the reassuring lump of handkerchief beneath her cuff.

'You think it's there. You can be so certain. It's supposed to be like yesterday.'

She'd forgotten me and spoke across me, not realising. I saw it, the smile her mouth was making, not quite able to hold.

'So young too,' she added, 'so young.'

So young, so young. The words are floating around inside her head. There's something else too she can almost remember, something the plate hasn't held, and she's struggling to think what. She deals through the other photographs and keeps returning to that one, the three of us at the party, Peter, her, and me between. Her memory's being lazy and muddy. She lifts the smiles to the light, she varies the angle. What is it?

I make a show of reading the Quicky-crossword clues in the *Telegraph*. Florence irks me like this, in her 'sentimental' moods, so much so I always want to leave the room, and I would do if I had the confidence I could get up enough steam. It's like acting: bad acting: hamming. I'm not going to be her audience.

'Twelve across,' I recite, in a voice just loud enough to carry my disregard, if she chooses to take it that way. 'Two words, four and eight. "Welcome far from ecstatic — hence mutton sandwiches?" '

*

She announced it after breakfast. 'Oh. We'll be having a guest.'

She slipped her hand down behind the carriage clock for the letter.

I composed myself to look politely interested, suspecting the worst. The term 'guest' is meant as a reproach: it blames me for my presence, for simply being here, occupying my square arthritic feet of every room, wherever Florence turns her head.

'Marjorie Campbell's coming. She's invited herself, although I did say. You don't mind? Remember Marjorie? Here's the letter. You can read it if you like. She wanders rather. She'll be no trouble. I'll air the little room.'

I didn't need the letter she handed me to remember. Marjorie Campbell was always Florence's friend: too sophisticated (in her own estimation) and too grown-up looking as a schoolgirl to care for a younger sister's company. After school she aged prematurely, as so many of our acquaintances did in the months and years following the War. I suppose that was the cruel fate which overtook those who could only give others and not themselves.

I remember too, from recent years, the acid twist to her mouth, the straight ramrod back, the legs clamped together, the armoury of pins stapled into the bun of silver hair, 'Our Lord' dropped into the conversation — now one of Florence's least endearing habits.

Marjorie Campbell's coming has occupied us for several days. Florence even sorted through the photographs again, taking the magnifying glass to the wedding groups, trying to make her out.

'I wanted her to be my bridesmaid. Do you remember? And she wouldn't. What a laugh!'

I remember what you don't, Florence: you in tears, saying you'd call everything off, Marjorie unrepentant, more confident than ever in the rightness of the deed, Mama appealed to and, operating at her diplomatic and placating level-best, restoring some kind of peace.

'You can't have forgotten, Elspeth, surely? Oh, it *was* a laugh, wasn't it?'

I watch you recalling more as you pass from room to room, straightening the pictures on the rails, smoothing the rugs flat with the toe of your shoe, smiling in the mirrors at yourself.

'Marjorie loved Peter, of course. I knew about it. I didn't have any doubts. She was jealous. Or is that what a wife . . . what any bride is going to think?'

I notice, Florence, how you stumble over the word 'wife' and the rest trails away. In the hall you open the coffer lid and look inside.

'Now, Elspeth dear, we'll need to use some of your space. For clothes, unders, odds and ends. Marjorie always had such lovely things, didn't she, I expect that's why people could find her attractive. If we could just juggle things around for a few days . . . And your wardrobe *is* bigger.'

Of course it is, of course it is. My sister silences me with another of her winning little sunburst smiles.

'Well, my bedroom's larger — marginally — isn't it? So we're square after all, Elspeth, aren't we?'

I can't do anything, and I wouldn't be allowed to — I'm only able to observe the preparations from my chair in front of the verandah window. I've felt the dullness returning to my bones of late, the hollow core of some pain that always seems too far away and too imprecise to place exactly. ('Psychosomatic', Florence mouths to her little circle when she thinks my back is turned.) My wrists and some of my fingers have swollen badly with the dampness and rain of last weekend. The two days since haven't helped, with an icy east wind we've both watched running rings round the meek, spineless conifer bushes in the gardens and playing havoc with the beach swings on the promenade.

The pain, when it comes, has a way of compressing me further and deeper into myself. Part of me wants to fight against it and deny it: but it's as if another worse 'self' I have no control over delights in the suffering, it luxuriates in anticipation at the prospect. Its joy is hearing the swings screech as their chains buckle and jump; it thrills when I stand where the wind seeps through a hair crack in the window's rubber sill and I feel as if rusty wires are pulling in my arms.

I offer to help, just to spite it. 'Maybe I could be of some help? Florence?'

Florence won't hear of it; she smiles down at me, pummelling the cushions behind my back with soft blows of her fist.

'Don't you trouble yourself, dear. You'll tell me if you're feeling a draught, won't you?'

She brushes past with a pile of linen tucked beneath her arm. I'm made conscious again of the utter shame of my position. In the evenings, when there isn't any avoiding each other, I look up and see Florence studying my hands and wrists across the dinner table: she pretends to be doing nothing of the sort, but I've already caught the expression of whatever it is, between embarrassment and irritation. Then there's a smile from her, a crack as her napkin is shaken out with a quick wrist flick, a sudden pre-occupation with the shininess or otherwise of the table silver.

The weather has obligingly cleared.

'Do you think we're going to have a St Luke's little summer, Elspeth?'

She's been at her patronising worst all morning. It's as much as I can do to steady the pen between my fingers.

'The promenade's quiet now. Do you hear, Elspeth? The promenade's quiet.' She speaks to me in the way people speak to defectives. 'Helen will be able to take you out, I'm sure. Wouldn't you like that?'

Her voice softens as it reminisces about another St Luke's little summer, in 1920.

'We couldn't have asked for more. Could we, Elspeth? "D.V." I told everyone, God's willed it. I really do believe it *must* have been meant for us. Don't you?'

In her memory she has no guilt at what she considers her happiness — even when, at odd moments, she's tried to imagine the loneliness of my single life. Peter and she were two selves in free communication: they knew how to make things work: taking what was granted them, the parable of the talents, one penny doubled, two pennies doubled, God helps those . . .

She lifts his photograph from the sideboard and rubs at the tortoiseshell frame with her duster. She speaks again, in her faraway reminiscing voice.

'I don't think Peter and I ever had any secrets from each other. Is that possible?'

Can she really believe that? — honestly and sincerely believe that?

My pen splutters a trickle of ink. A globule gathers at the end of the nib.

'I think I've left the blotter in my room,' I say to her very quietly.

Then comes the understanding pat on my wrist. There are dire patches like this in every day — each time Florence lapses into one of these exasperatingly high-sounding, mawkish moods — when I think, truly I could learn to despise my sister.

Florence

So it continued all morning, and the letter finally had to be abandoned. At lunchtime a man's voice on the radio told them that the wind had blown itself out. Florence, waiting for Helen to arrive, tried to look cheered.

'You'll be able to get out.'

She glanced over at Elspeth's two helpless wrists.

'When Helen comes. She can walk down with you. If you like. It seems a pity not to take advantage of what we're given.'

She smiled pleasantly, rolling back the windows on to the balcony.

'These little lulls.'

Helen was late and had to wait for the end of the 'Woman's Hour' serial before Elspeth would get herself ready. Florence realised she was being 'difficult'. When they were at the door, just about to start out, she changed her mind about what to wear and went back to her room and put on another coat. She had to get another pair of gloves because she'd laid one of the woollen ones down and couldn't think where. Then they couldn't find Pa's cane; Florence spotted it on the balcony, hanging from the strip of trellis, and presented it to her with what she meant to be great tact.

'Well, I hope you have a nice walk. Elspeth, Helen. Both of you. There's a sun up there somewhere!'

She pulled a wisp of hair back with tanned, mobile fingers. She saw Elspeth studying the liver-marks that covered her own hands like a lizard's mottled skin as she eased her fingers into the cold leather gloves.

'A brisk blow, Elspeth dear. And I'll have tea ready when you get back.'

Florence watched them leave from the balcony. She waved after them. There were times when she could feel unutterably sad for her sister: there were times too when she felt much less, when the lack of gratitude, the gracelessness, seemed to drain the energy out of her. There were moments when she quite dreaded the prospect of what lay ahead of them, the years they would spend closeted together, walled up. (Helen had been calculated on as a temporary insurance against that final, desperate isolation.) Sometimes she was just plain irritated: on their worst days Elspeth gave nothing back, grudging each of her pleasantries, still pretending life had plenty of other possibilities open to her.

Tiredly Florence slid the glass panel shut behind her and made her way through the sitting-room towards the hall. She suddenly felt despondent enough for tears, but realised she must fight them back, she mustn't give in.

It wasn't how she'd intended it should be, any of it. Somehow or other she and Elspeth were to have drawn closer together. She'd imagined age closing in on them both, but not claustrophobically, not as a burden: it was to have been something very different, a kind of tender and warming reflection of that privileged and sun-drenched girlhood they'd shared together behind 'Trebetherick's' tended hedges and crumbling honeystone walls, in their innocent years.

Instead . . . They lived by their little white lies. Her own sweet concern. All Elspeth's talk of what she *might* do in her last years —

painting, flower-pressing, going off to visit her friends in Havant and Shropshire, seeing Torquay or the ruins at Knossos — if only she chose to do so.

She couldn't blame Elspeth entirely: the distortions of reality weren't all hers, she hadn't a monopoly of them. In her own memories, she was only too aware, she'd never passed beyond that mythical summer of 1914. The autumn had splintered that dream, scattering whatever hopes they might have had: and in some way it had cleft *them* apart too, two sisters, an iron wedge had been driven between them (like a walnut and its shell, or an acorn and its cup, their mother used to laugh after them, watching the hatching of some conspiracy in the garden).

Her impressions would always begin to fade as the summer itself had faded, leaving the two of them alone — herself and Elspeth — and with too little to do in that great gaunt house with its fusty-smelling rooms and silent, unlit corridors. She remembered listening to the floorboards creaking and groaning as she lay curled up in bed at night, unable to sleep, and the gas in the pretty fluted porcelain bracket next to the wardrobe hissing and throwing wild shadows on to the ceiling. But she remembered so little of what followed, with Pa and Geoffrey dead and two brass plates screwed to the wall in church — that nothing-time when the orchard became tumbledown, and the grass fringing the lawn grew too high, and the panes of glass rattled dangerously in the conservatory roof whenever she tried to clear a path through the debris of neglect, snatching at cobwebs and the dead men's legs of plants strangled and withered in their pots.

The only certainty left to her had been themselves, she and Elspeth, the two Mercer girls. But then, quite suddenly — after the summers of arms linked around each other's waists, and the confidences in the summer-house, and the jokes worked on their friends — Elspeth had changed. She remembered a certain look of pale-faced alarm that would appear on her face, and the brief edgy replies when she dared to ask her questions across the breakfast table, and long moody afternoons when she wouldn't speak at all, preferring her own company to her sister's, reading alone upstairs in her bedroom. There had been nothing to explain it. Mother would return in the evenings, looking fragile and drawn from the responsibilities of whichever charity she'd pledged herself to: Elspeth would brighten a little then, she'd close the book in her hand for a short while, but afterwards she'd pale again, to something like her mother's shadow, and the three of them would settle to the privacy of their occupations in their three dim corners of the gassy sitting-room.

She found herself back at the window, watching Elspeth and Helen as they made their slow, decent way up the drive, saying nothing, leaning together into the wind. Helen lent an arm and Elspeth folded hers through the crook, pulling her coat (black, from a time when the colour was fashionable) closer about her. As she watched, the arm's grasp grew tighter on Helen's, seeming to hold her back, slowing her. The pace was Elspeth's as, very precisely, they took the shallow steps up to the top lawn. Around their feet the wind sent a snake of leaves swirling in a fast, scampering circle. The trees cradled themselves, empty-armed, against the wind's buffetings.

Once before on a 'bad' afternoon it had happened, the trees huddling inconsolably over their shame had weakened her to these same dry tears she could now feel pricking and sticking behind her eyes. Confusedly, for a moment, they were different trees, 'Trebetherick's' famous elms, marshalled into a shady walk, which had run from the side of the house to one of the rusted iron gates into the fields. Something had happened once, she and Peter had finished the honeymoon trip, they were driving back to the house, to Elspeth and Mother: she'd seen the desecration from a couple of hundred yards away, the dismal row of lopped trunks, standing in stupid, uncomprehending dismay. At the house Elspeth had merely smiled at her anger and breathless outburst, then pulled a face and calmly turned her back on her. 'Of course, my dear Florence, it's very easy to decide what's to be done if one goes gallivanting off for a couple of months!' She'd opened her mouth to reply to her but, before the words could fly out, Peter had put his arm on hers and was leading her into the hall. It was over, it was done, he told her: what had happened had happened, and that was that. She'd just looked at him, blankly: that most certainly was not that, she said, couldn't he understand? She tried to explain to him as they began unpacking in their room how, in their faraway lands, she'd pictured the trees as she'd expected to find them: pacing the walk between them, touching the trunks with her fingers wide, stroking the mossy bark, passing from one remembered shape and mass to another. After they'd finished, before dinner, when she was calmer, she took him outside. The sun blazing into their eyes was shires away. They followed the path to the fields, trailing their long shadows on the damp grass. The sky had narrowed to vapid thin streamers of light, tatters of pink, lemon, cornflower blue. They walked between the hacked trees, stopping, moving on from one to the next to the next.

'It's criminal,' she told him. She wanted to cry. 'Insane.'

'We should be sorry for her,' was Peter's reply.

'What about the trees, then?' Her voice was high and raspy. 'What about *them*?' They at least could feel the smart, she assured him.

'Why can't you see?' she asked him. 'Why can't you see what she's done?'

And in the pincushion of her heart she felt a vicious little pain, a needle stab — and for a few seconds an intensity of coldness burned there, like an injection of ice.

Sixty years later Elspeth's behaviour was still a mystery to her. Now she must be content to leave it at that.

'She's got a right to her own life, in her imagination,' she would tell her few confidential friends — Celia, Bunty, Frances. 'And she's had to suffer so much. I mean, physically.'

She would try to convince herself it was only compensation for the confinement Elspeth must be feeling in the flat. She explained it to her friends almost every time she rang them up; she would pause between cryptic sentences while Elspeth made her way stiffly from the room, making another noble demonstration of Not Hearing Anything.

'Helen, of course, has been a wonder. I don't know what I'd ever have done without her.'

Her friends, in their turn, congratulated her.

'You've done everything, Florence. We're so full of admiration. You and Helen. It's a happy home. That will always be your consolation. Knowing you've done everything.'

Sister and sister.

And 'blood', as she was forever reminding her friends, 'is thicker than water'.

Remembering Helen and the shopping list and the library books as she evened up the arrangement of dried flowers on the pembroke table in the hall, she thought of her mother — her submissiveness, and how she would always apply herself to any task in hand so that it became a point of honour with her to get it done.

She opened the door of Elspeth's room and went in, willing herself into the mood for another cleaning bee.

She began tidying the clutter on the dressing-table, very quickly: handkerchiefs, the tub of talcum powder without its lid, a lipstick without its case, umpteen emery boards. She rearranged the silver-topped bottles and the silver-backed brushes that had sat on their mother's dressing-table, and her mother's before her. 'And all this,' she couldn't help the thought, 'to look as we do.' She picked up the heirlooms of trumpery, dusting beneath them, feeling in herself the wisdom of centuries. 'We are born with nothing, and we leave with nothing.' And leaving these baubles and geegaws behind, she wondered, lifting the bottles up and examining them as she screwed their tops on straight, to whom do we leave them? — to their cousin's uncaring son on his Flinders Island sheep farm, to his Melbourne wife Jayleen they'd never seen? She felt, as she always felt, saddened at the prospect.

She'd lived with this same sadness for fifty years, knowing there might have been someone: a child. Might have been.

She tugged at the wardrobe door, and it rattled open. Dresses and coats she'd never had a chance to investigate hung drooping on their hangers. A mothball dropped off the sill and rolled on to the floor. She didn't see it and stepped back, crushing it with her heel.

She wrinkled her nose and tried to concentrate on what she had to do. Some of the clothes, most of them, hadn't been out of the wardrobe in the nine months. The dresses and coats would have to be sorted through. They hung on their shallow mahogany yokes as if they'd been fated to always slouch from tired old bones.

She pushed the few empty hangers along to the other end of the rail, puzzling where Marjorie's things were to go. She'd had to make apologies in her letters for the lack of storage space. 'You'll find us so cramped. An awful lot had to be got rid of, of course.' At the beginning, before the move, she'd had to ask Elspeth to be very particular about what she was bringing with her. Elspeth had been rather less than gracious about it, not seeming to realise that sacrifices were involved on both sides. (There'd been so much she'd wanted to keep about her too and hadn't been able to, had Elspeth not seen that?: the drawing-room furniture from home, the paintings, her share of their father's porcelain, Peter's Chinese things from his navy days.) Elspeth, typically, had swerved from one extreme of obtuseness and perversity to the other, and sold more or less everything she had. 'The money has nothing to do with it, Florence,' she'd haughtily informed her over the phone from Phillips on the day of the sale. 'That doesn't mean a thing to me.' ('*It can't buy me back my independence*,' she'd written in letters to her friends and confidantes in Havant and Shropshire, and Florence had read the remark over her shoulder.)

It came back to her as she knelt down and began raking among the shoes and wads of tissue paper. She pulled out some empty cardboard boxes and stacked them beside her.

Elspeth would just have to try her best, she'd tell her so: fit things in where she could.

She started on the shoes, pulling them out and laying them in pairs behind the boxes. On most of them the gold Rayne and Bally

Suisse signatures were hardly worn at all. Her eyebrows met, in disapproval. Elspeth had always spent extravagantly on her feet. 'People invariably forget all about their shoes,' their mother had instructed them during one of her lecturing sessions. 'They think nobody sees, that feet don't matter, down there. You should begin with your feet: if your feet are comfortable, you naturally assume a proper poise.' Mother's gift had been to make such 'bons mots' of advice sound convincing. But, Florence considered, somehow or other those particular ones hadn't quite worked with Elspeth, although she'd tried hard enough to achieve, the poise part, She'd decided long ago that it was at the other end of Elspeth's person that the troubles really began, inside her head, and in some way the pain in her limbs and joints only derived from that.

She had her arms round Elspeth's lead-bellied ditty box, dented with being dropped so often that the lid wouldn't shut, and she was dragging it out when the weight of it made her lose her balance, the strength in her arms snapped — and the box crashed upside down on to the floor.

Awkwardly she hauled herself up off her hands and felt the weakness shuddering up her arms to her shoulders. She sank back on her heels. Just occasionally — like this — her system had a hiccup and it was as if for a few seconds she lost her confidence too, and her control slipped from her. She tried not to think about that now.

She began picking the correspondence up in handfuls — bills, receipts, postcards, lawyers' letters on the thick cream sheets she remembered from her grandfather's time. Her eyes swept over the cascade of paper. So much to legitimise the life of just one person: the pain echoing across her shoulders made it all seem, for once, pathetic, desperate even.

She pulled herself up. For a few moments she sat with her legs tucked untidily and uncomfortably beneath her and started spreading out the fans of paper with the tips of her fingers.

She wasn't attending when something caught her eye, layers beneath the red and amber postcards of Baden and Cassis and the crisp London solicitors' letters with their richly embossed, confidence-inspiring references. She'd seen a line, a phrase, a word — it might have been upside-down but she couldn't have been mistaken about it, knowing that round and open and generous script as well as she knew her own and the jammed-together, lean-to, thorn-bush kind Elspeth wrote.

She unscrambled the layers, lifting the papers up in sheaves till she found it. She singled it out, picked it up. She hesitated for a moment or two, weighing the letter in her hand.

Then — already a little alarm bell was ringing in her head — she started to read it.

It was from Peter. Dated about the time he first came calling at the house in the fields, months before he attempted to turn her thoughts to marriage. She skipped a few lines, read some more. Her eyes flew up to the top line: it was for Elspeth. It wasn't something he'd written for her which had gone astray.

'*Elspeth darling, my love . . .*'

She was conscious enough to feel the blood flaring in her face, singing behind her ears. The lines swam suddenly, tilted, dipped, ran into each other. The letter fluttered from her fingers and floated to the floor.

Time passed, and again she was conscious — of herself, herself in the room kneeling on the floor, and the letter lying beside her on the rug.

Slowly she picked it up. She held it lightly this time, scarcely at all, between her fingertips.

The paper was crinkled with reading and re-reading. The years had faded the black ink to the coppery crimson of words on her father's old letters home from France, like trails of dried blood.

She felt her brain, the thoughts in her head, freezing over. Then somehow she was back on her feet, she was standing up again. She was trying not to think, not to think.

Very hesitantly, unsurely, she began to retrace her steps backwards. Not able to help herself thinking, half-remembering, grasping at places, moments, faces, movements across a room.

The memories had no shape, no density, they were wisps of cotton wool teased out of a round, massless ball. There was something else, some too vague recollection, sounds — a squeaking floorboard, someone laughing, a smothered cry — trickling down at her from an upstairs bedroom.

And then for a long time — minutes on end, half an hour, like a hole in the day she'd dropped into — there was nothing.

She found she was sitting on the edge of the bed. She looked dully at the bedside table, not seeing things (but remembering them later), a Breton lace handkerchief that had been her mother's or her grandmother's, an embroidered bookmark, the clean pad of notepaper, Elspeth's red leather diary with its shiny gilt lock.

Outside she was aware of the prim whirring of the gardener's mower, splitting the tenses now/then: aware of the respectability of their landscaped and double-glazed lives, herself sitting here and — behind the screen of rhododendrons — the sea and its tarmacadam'd promenade. She had a picture of Elspeth being assisted carefully (Helen's arm on her arm) as far as the little pier, where the pleasure boats left from and returned to, which jutted itself defiantly into the wide arc of the bay. She also thought forwards: to Elspeth's return, Helen hovering in the hall taking her time to remove her gloves and not wanting to intrude. The three of them having to begin all over again . . .

She looked at the floor. She looked at her shoes at the ends of her legs, the weave of her skirt, the letter clutched again between her fingers.

'*My own dearest Elspeth . . .*'

Like one of Shelley's letters she'd pored over beneath its glass cover in the tiny museum in the town, the fadings of the ink should have worn the sentiment to a kind of parody of real feeling, a quaint historical whim: love with its sting drawn.

Her eyebrows drew together. She studied the surface details of the letter, she concentrated on them as a bibliographical scholar might: the pricks of dampness in the margin, rust spots on the politely worded passion, the brown windsor rim running along the top of the sheet, the uneven fading of the ink, fainter on one half of the page than on the other, lightening in places almost to nothing. The signature ended with a flourish and a long upward stroke: the other letters — the 'P' in particular, the open loop curling devil-may-care on its stave — were more flamboyant than she would have remembered. The words had been written quickly, but in the way Peter had always thought of as having to do with 'Style', his own version of eighteenth-century script with heroic, expansive sweeps and links.

What about the writer of the letter? Her understanding seemed to be clearing second by second as she read more.

She didn't need a scholar's judgement to tell her this had been a man too keen to impress. Only someone who didn't really know himself, didn't know his own mind, could have written these fancy words. A man sweet-talking his way with false persuasions, who was only covering over the disgrace of his emptiness inside . . .

Thinking it, she felt she betrayed them all — Elspeth, herself, and Peter worst of all.

She shut her eyes. How had Elspeth reacted? Not how she had done herself later: falling for it, a trick she didn't have the quickness to see, which she hadn't even suspected might not be the thing he called it when he whispered in her ear, 'love' . . .

She stood up very suddenly. She did a little tour of the room. She touched objects with her fingers. She looked out the window. She saw nothing at first, then adjusted and focused as the gardener started to move across her line of vision, behind his lawn-mower.

No, she thought with a rush of bitterness into her head, Elspeth hadn't deviated, *she* hadn't been deflected at all: Elspeth had read his nature as she, his own wife, had only begun — once or twice, very guiltily, in the middle of the night, in the darkness of her most private thoughts — to half-surmise. (But not even that; now she saw she hadn't been capable of guessing the merest thing about this man who'd let her marry him . . .)

The letter fell from her hand and again it fluttered to the floor. The gardener's mower had stopped. In the silence she found herself remembering something else — quite distinctly now — that had been lost to her or suppressed since the thing had happened. It was as clear to her as if she was watching a colour film on television. It belonged to the time when she and Peter were at the stage of being just polite friends but when aunts and uncles and Mother's circle were already voicing their 'expectations' in their hearing. One hot, still, breathless afternoon in June or July in the garden at home, a moment of intense quiet at siesta time, she'd been coming back up from the strawberry frames when they'd stepped out on to the cinder path in front of her, Peter and Elspeth (who could only have been seventeen or eighteen). They hadn't noticed her, and she'd fallen a little behind, from embarrassment rather than because she'd wanted to see, to know, anything. (So, then, *had* she suspected?) She'd looked back at the knoll they'd come sliding down from, at the little summer-house on its rotating platform on the top. The doors were open; the room was dark inside, but she could see that the cushions had been built up on the old sagging chaise longue. Their footsteps trailed away into the middle distance, neither of them was speaking: there was no laughing, no singing in the ha-ha funny way she was used to hearing from them. Sunshine, she could remember, had never seemed so sombre nor so reflective before: she was feeling slightly sick, and maybe she'd reeled a little on her feet. A pigeon had flapped overhead and clattered into the cover of the copse, finding the shadows.

She crouched on the Bukhara rug, in the middle of Elspeth's bedroom floor, stooped over the letters, picking them up and piling them into the ditty box.

She was seeing the days ahead, and what was coming to them: the masked politenesses, attending with extra special closeness to the little things, the moment-to-moment actions, so that she wouldn't have to say anything, she wouldn't have to look. And the nights — the dreams broken open, the endless hypotheses that would keep her awake while the radio voice quietly warbled beside her on the bedside table and Elspeth lay sleepless in her own bed, only inches away behind the wall.

She pushed the rest into the box, bills and holiday postcards and envelopes with 'Havant' and 'Ludlow' postmarks. She forced the lid shut, fumbling with the clasp, and pulled herself slowly and painfully to her feet. An old woman was clambering to her feet in the dressing-table mirror on the other side of the room.

They smiled together — conspirators' smiles — but all she saw was the sadness in them.

The other smile emptied itself slowly. She watched the lips pull together as she'd watched Elspeth's pucker nervously for the last nine months. She reminded herself with a school-mistress's severe caution that there would be no outward difference in her behaviour or in her appearance.

She looked down and tidied the rumples in her skirt, smoothing the creases. She straightened her back, she ran a hand over her hair. Her fingers fidgeted with her collar.

The shock, she knew, should have been more than it was. She should have been feeling any number of emotions, not this: not this simple, solemn care to record her impressions or their lack.

She examined herself critically in the mirror, turning a three-quarters circle and back again.

Maybe she had begun to suspect, maybe not: in a sense — incredible to imagine — it hardly mattered one way or the other, not now.

Instead she was aware of herself becoming calmer as the minutes passed — and, curiously, more confident of what would be.

She knew that at least she'd outlived the likelihood of ever being sufficiently shocked by any event to want to vent her personality — as this situation might have seemed to demand — on another person. 'If it happened' — she adjusted the cuffs of her blouse — 'it was meant to happen. And that must be that.'

The woman looked back at her with a momentary despair in her eyes.

She turned her back on her, wanting to concentrate on something so trivial she wouldn't feel more of this determination ebbing from her. She leaned across the bed and pulled the cover straight. She smoothed the lump of the pillow. After the first War and everything that had happened to them, she'd known there could be nothing like melodrama again. And the same truth, she was telling herself, must still hold. She'd lived a life without histrionics, the passionate contrasts between states she'd observed in other people: she'd missed out on a good deal perhaps, but she'd protected herself from what she had always foreseen would be worse risks.

She opened the door and took a last look round the bedroom. On Saturday there would be Marjorie, and the business would begin in earnest, having to pretend to them both that her life was quite contented and complete just as it was.

In the corridor she tapped on the barometer window as she always did in passing. The needle wavered on the thin line between 'Fair' and 'Changeable'. She caught herself off-guard, smiling even at the information on the oval glass. And then she thought of everything she had to do before Saturday, and ran an unseeing eye over Helen's long list on the pembroke table.

They'd both be back again soon. She tidied her hair in the hallstand mirror, carefully with both hands, and made tracks towards the kitchen. Tea, two slivers of Celia's Dundee cake, the box of biscuits Bunty had brought them. Helen making busy noises in the dining-room. The attempt at communication.

'How was your walk? You've got the colour back into your cheeks, anyway.'

She held the kettle beneath the cold tap, looking out the window. Across the lawns she could see them, Helen halting, Elspeth scrutinising the turf, feigning a vital interest. The wind scooped the leaves around their feet, catching them both in a tight circle. She turned the tap off and slammed the kettle on to the ring louder than she'd meant.

Back at the window, straightening her cuffs, she watched their hesitant approach. They'd reached the elm path. Someone in the flats who knew about these things had told them that in eight or nine months probably every tree in the windbreak would be dead. In their brochure the builders had made it a feature of the place, a survival from a bygone age when there'd been only one house of mansion proportions on the site. Soon, like the famous elm walk at home it would be just a kind of fiction, another little victory owing to the past.

She turned back to the cooker and lit the gas, watching the flame splay beneath the kettle and remembering how the bedroom in her mother's house used to smell at night. Already, she wondered, *they* were being phased out of the system too, she and Elspeth, as anachronisms? — and this was how it began? This constant reduction. After a time, maybe, when it was too late for anything else, one meekly accepted it. It was the reward — from God — for having had what one did. Paying for the pleasures: the final reckoning, the totting up and taking away.

That thought somehow comforted her, as she stood resting her hip on the cooker waiting for the kettle to whistle to the boil.

It comes only once. And whatever it had been — 'it', 'life', 'experience', every single thing that had contributed — it *had been*, and nothing could alter that now.

Downstairs, the front door, caught by the wind and pulled out of their hands, banged shut behind the walkers. Two floors up, Florence prepared herself, turning off the gas beneath the kettle. She picked up the cake tin and eased off the lid, making an instant mental division of Celia's Dundee cake into how many pieces. Her instincts, she reminded herself, weren't going to fail her now.

She tipped out the cake and slid it on to a plate. She wasn't, after all — and would never be — alone, as alone as Elspeth. And then she remembered the blood, the inside chemistry, the knot of kin there was no undoing: and it came to her, *that* was the truth of it all, and it was why she was continuing to go through the motions, making the tea, and why in the weakness and indignity of age she would outlast any shock that came to her. The blood was what they never saw, and it was everything. It still surged around inside them, elemental and abstractly complex at the same time. It was a symbol of their closeness — their biology was the same —

and simultaneously of their apart-ness, since the blood occupied two quite separate bodies.

They were sisters, she heard her neighbours say they were 'close'. Speaking to them or to her friends she sometimes came out with the adage 'blood is thicker than water'. What *did* it mean? Perhaps it meant that, to death, one possessed part of the other? — in their fleshy manufacture, in conscience, and in memory? The union went back to the womb, and the same bloody water they'd swum in, and the geography of a darkly private place they were the only two alive to have known . . .

Apart and together.

Their mutual trust in the same man betrayed.

The key blundered in the lock, and she finished rubbing her fingers dry on the dish towel. Later there would be time to think and reconsider: time and enough, all the time she could possibly need.

She checked her appearance again, shook the creases free, coaxed back the loose wisps of hair. She practised a smile in the cooker fascia, not really seeing herself properly. She heard the voices congratulating themselves on safe home, and she tried to float in on their wavelength. The words she would use came to her and she re-ordered them so that they would sound gentler and more caring than usual.

She sensed the pressure shifting on the timbers under the overlay of parquet as they came looking for her.

'Here!' she called to them. 'In here!'

She reached for the door handle and felt herself concentrating the rest of her life into the sudden dazzle brightness of her smile.

Endpiece

I've heard it said that our life stories have already been written for us — and all we do is act them out.

This is a tale to be kept for night: when the moon shines in on an ornamental garden, or the rain beats down on a blasted heather moor.

I shall tell you of history. I shall tell you of these years that are conveniently termed our 'present' time, the 1940s. Days and nights of living on the edge: never trusting the ceiling to last standing till the morning, not being sure if the loose stone flags of the pavement will hold your weight — or pull apart and down you fall.

Follow the line back, to its source . . . Believe me, if you can.

Late one foggy afternoon — it was the second of November, 1942, All Souls' Day — I was sitting in the 'Pandora' Tea Rooms in down-at-heels Holborn, where I was rooming at that time.

I had my notepad open on the table (beside my gasmask case, which is another detail of these days), but no ideas were coming to me, none at all.

I should explain, if I really can. Not about the writing part, or wanting to write (since I hadn't been published yet). I mean, about how I'd been caught in a blast during the most recent raid of the War on London. That I had a blank, a black hole, when I tried to remember that event and my terrible time in hospital, first on a life support, then in intensive care, finally the desperate weeks in 'solitary' when they put me on the librium treatment. On the effects of that I'd run off on a moonlight flight, back to the city — sped there with my head swimming and not seeming to be a part of me at all. It was only now, still very dazed and woozy, that I was beginning to piece together a sort of life for myself, half-dead and half-alive as I was. For weeks I'd felt I was drifting, in a haze of half-remembrance . . .

I *do* remember this, that the tea they served in 'Pandora's' that All Souls' Day while I sat dreaming was tarry and deadly to swallow. Nor can I forget that someone had left a copy of the London *Times* on a table, for that was how it began . . .

I salvaged the newspaper and turned to the 'Domestic Situations' column as was my wont and let my eyes go wandering ahead of my thoughts. There on the page I was suddenly waylaid by an announcement in a box someone had ringed with blue ink: advertising for the services of a young woman with 'proven secretarial abilities' to act as a lady's 'companion-cum-social-secretary' in her new home.

A telephone number was included, and I went outside to a phone box and called with the last coins in my purse. At the other end the receiver was lifted from its cradle and a maid spoke to me. I found next I was talking to the mistress of the house. She seemed quite unsurprised by my call. She addressed me in elderly, mandarin tones.

'My name,' she said — and hesitated — 'is Mrs Drake.'

Had I taken note of the position advertised? she asked. Please would I be so obliging as to state a time when I could make my way to Number Seven, Shilling Passage, Chelsea?

I memorised the queer address. She said 'good-bye'. I repeated her. The line went dead in my ear, b-r-r-r-r, and I replaced the receiver.

Back inside 'Pandora's' I scribbled her name down in my notepad half-a-dozen times and I noticed — for some reason it gave me a little jolt of astonishment — that if you transposed two of the letters what you spelt was 'Mrs *Darke*'.

Another realisation struck me on the way home: that she'd used my name and for the life of me I couldn't be certain that I'd actually spoken the words to tell her.

* * *

Behind Cheyne Walk, in the confusion of dog's leg alleyways and cobbled cul-de-sacs of Old Chelsea, it's like being in a quaintly angled sea port. That's the 'feel' of those backwaters. At least it was in Anno Domini 1942, on November days with the fog creeping up from the river and an oily sea smell everywhere which was forever clinging to your hair and clothes — and always the murk of the afternoon streets, pricked by blue sizzling gas lamps. It made you think of wreckers and their wicked flares.

In Shilling Passage I was received in the shadowy first-floor drawing-room in a high Hogarthian house as tall as a schooner. Rising from her chair to meet me, Mrs Drake showed herself to be rather hawkish and oriental, in the manner of the artsy women of Bloomsbury of the 1920s. In flagrant disregard of the alternative name I'd given her, Mrs 'Darke', she was wearing brilliant hues of marine blue (turquoise and amethyst predominated: her shoes were coloured summer-sky blue and her turban was shot with peacock tones).

By way of introduction she explained to me in a pianissimo voice that her own house had been flattened during a raid, and here she was — quote — 'a kind of tenant'. (I nodded my head, I attempted to look knowledgeable and sympathetic. I knew she meant that in effect she was 'rooming', like me.) I would not be required to live here, but I must be 'to hand'. (I inclined my head again, but my nod didn't betoken my full understanding.) I would be a sort of 'go-between' — between 'here' and (she pointed outside) 'there'.

She advanced towards the door. It opened just before she reached it — the handle turned — and the maid noiselessly stepped in with tea things (black Wedgwood) set out on a tray. (I must tell you that every gesture and movement in that house was performed silently.)

I forgot my Holborn doubts as I was served with the thin brew in a black cup and saucer — 'chrysanthemum tea', my hostess informed me — and a petit-beurre biscuit. We both sat down and then we set to discussing the matter of my secretarial 'qualifications', which I have to say did not properly exist (no more than my ideas had an existence or substance yet in the pages of literary journals, which it was my ambition in life to achieve.)

Mrs Drake must have liked me, or she must have seen some promise in me, or found my fictional account of my skills and experience convincing. When she asked her final question of me — would I care to accept an offer of employment? — I had no wish to decline and said 'yes, indeed!', without allowing myself a second thought.

So it was that I was taken on that same day. I 'joined the ship', as it were.

* * *

The bomb which had dropped on Mrs Drake/Darke in the latter days of the War had destroyed all her papers. I discovered that before anything else. Now it appeared that, like me, she was beginning the long process of piecing together an existence.

One of my first functions was despatching change-of-address cards. These were very discreet, although quirkily edged with black. Attending to them (sustained by frequent servings of chrysanthemum tea from the collied china pot) was office-work, but I imagined I could do it unthinkingly: that wasn't quite the case, because it was a finicky, particular business involving lists and cross-checking — rather like a jig-saw puzzle, a pastime I've never been patient enough nor had the sort of memory for.

We worked together in the dining-room on the task, with telephone and street directories laid open on top of the mahogany table to help us find some of the addresses, which I would then jot down in my notepad. (A considerable proportion of the entries we were looking for were either 'ex-' or now missing. So very many names too, yet why — it occurred to me after a fortnight or so — why was it always the same few friends who called to visit, pale faces that flitted apologetically past me up and down stairs?)

Whose house is *this* one? I wanted to ask her to break the monotony sometimes, but couldn't steel myself to do just yet. For how long are you bound to be a tenant here, 'rooming' as grandly as you contrive to?

We said very little to one another, though — on that topic or any other — and what we did say I've forgotten. I do remember us sitting among gilt pier-glasses of another age. I would see ourselves reflected dozens of times — dozens of ourselves — looking misty and ethereal. I also remember that the room smelt of beeswax and pot pourri heaped in wide shallow bowls. It was a dark room — the walls were olive green and velvet drapes of a deeper green half-hid the windows — and even when the table-lamps were switched on I had to strain my eyes to see on those dim, silent November afternoons of wartime 1942 when we drank chrysanthemum tea from the antique black Wedgwood pot and, outside, the river fog came swirling up the Chelsea lanes and passageways.

* * *

I knew that Mrs Drake's/Darke's original house had been lost. (I went and double-checked: there was a hole a-gape in the maw of the elegant street in Kensington, like a tooth knocked out. Only that one house, so selective had fate been.) I didn't realise till I consulted official records and old newspapers that, in addition, several lives had been lost: seven all told. (I speculated, maybe a dinner party had just got going as the bomb came roaring out of the sky?) Two of the bodies — the war coroner's report read 'possibly female' — had been too charred to merit positive proof of identification. There were no recorded survivors from the night it happened, but I knew that in London at that date there had been all sorts of miracles of endurance being spoken of, so why not Mrs Drake's/Darke's too?

The next day I plucked up courage and put some prepared question to my employer about the bomb falling, remembering my own experience of months before. Immediately she gave me a brilliant blast of a smile, whose coldness reached me across the room. 'What can I say?' she replied, with such a semblance of reasonableness and in a tone of voice that seemed meant to be intimate.

I would have pursued the topic, but something dissuaded me in the next few seconds as I sat calculating: maybe the fear that she knew I had no secretarial skills and I had lied to her, that perhaps I could not hope to hide my evasions from her: that I had literary ambitions which I hadn't disclosed to her and which were intended to be my guarantee of immortality: that — to suit the immediate circumstances — I'd invented myself into being a certain person 'apart' and it was solely for her benefit.

* * *

On our afternoons dealing with the black-bordered cards I started watching her closely. I became astonished by her reflexes and instincts and puzzled why I hadn't noticed before, why I'd failed to pick up what was now so obvious. So obvious and so strange.

This, for instance: she would be up on her feet seconds *before* the front-door bell rang. Or this: she would close the gap for ventilation between the window sash and the sill just *before* the roving dogs came howling along the Embankment. From the middle of a pile of loose sheets of paper she would retrieve exactly the one she required, her eyes alighting on a particular name and address. If I couldn't find something she would tell me it was in this drawer or that, or wedged behind the chiffonier, or kicked beneath a rug, or even that it was in my burberry pocket — and there, wherever she said, unfailingly I would find it.

* * *

I can't recall now when it was, in the soupy half-light of those days, that I became prey to a bizarre thought: that Mrs Drake/Darke was not properly of this world, as I'd always accepted it.

She idly picked up the base of the telephone one afternoon, chatting to me over her shoulder — *then* it rang in her hands and she lifted the receiver and started talking into it, quite unconcerned, to one of her pallid, bloodless friends who frequented the house.

Another afternoon she went up and down the steep stairs checking for something or other and, while I sat in the dining-room listening for sounds and just able to see out on to the landing as she passed and re-passed, I didn't once hear a door squeak open or shut or a single floorboard groan in the structure of that ancient house, tall and stately as a sailing ship now landlocked high-and-dry in Chelsea.

I couldn't rid myself of the thought — that my employer might even be deceased, in the 'beyond' — and it seemed to possess me. In my surer moments I did consider that some of those incidents could be explained as coincidence — nothing more untoward at work than the principles of chance — but scientific confidence is a very devil to hold on to, let me tell you . . .

One morning I didn't make my usual journey to Chelsea on the bus: and that was that. I decided I would never return to that house. At the same time I couldn't understand why my fancy had such a grip of me. (During the early part of the War I'd done my practical bit in a munitions factory and I'd been able to believe then that my destiny would be of my own making thereafter; I would be a 'modern woman', I would be fulfilled. I'd believed that fiction till the bomb fell and concussed me, in the same week of blitz strikes that had claimed Mrs Drake's/Darke's house and the seven lives inside it.)

Lying low in my room in Holborn, supine under a temporary ceiling, I felt this was not at all how a 'modern woman' ought to be behaving. I was thinking things I ought not to be, I held my head in my hands with my fingers spread to try *not* to think, to cage my mind.

* * *

I didn't go back. Technically I was in the wrong: I hadn't told her, and I was owing her my time. But how could I be 'owing' anything to a person who might only be a fleeting tenant of the terrestrial? I also consoled myself with the thought that the money I'd been paid for my services — crisp banknotes inside sealed envelopes — that was real at least: wasn't it?

I shortly had cause to wonder. For in that dark season of no work — and so little chance of work for those of my kind — my funds diminished with alarming speed. At last they threatened to vanish completely, into thin air, just like a conjurer's trick.

I wondered on cold, drizzly days of little hope if I might not be letting go of my senses. I befriended the Javanese shadow puppets propped up in the dusty window of a curiosity-shop which I passed daily on my route to the British Museum Reading Room, where I laboured on my stories. I asked myself, had I ever really met those intimates of hers I'd thought I'd been introduced to? — the violinist, the Right Honourable gentleman, the tipsy poet, the former society hostess with scarlet nails like talons. As they'd gone brushing past me (and the maid on tip-toe) in the narrow hall of the house, had they been alive or dead — in this world or in another?

* * *

I waited for the fog, one of those days when it would linger from dawn till the bells of midnight, then I made my way back to Chelsea in the middle of that afternoon.

Just to look.

At last I found Shilling Passage, after a couple of wrong-turnings, past a newly-erected hoarding with the words 'Life Holdings of London Limited' stencilled on it. I pulled my burberry collar up, against the cold and damp. I'd been watching the house's unlit windows for several minutes when I realised with a start that a figure was watching me from the dining-room on the first floor where we'd worked. It was standing well back in the gloom. I tugged at the knot of my headscarf; and then — it was only then — I began to shake, quite uncontrollably.

* * *

Now winter's lurking in the city, like a hunched beast, and I wonder if I have the makings of a writer at all.

The dim yellow lights shine out of 'Pandora's' on to the street's greasy tarmacadam. Occasionally a car passes with its headlamps on, wheel wings gleaming, tyres hissing on the wet.

I wonder how everything is to be caught — stayed — wrought into a woof of words.

The other customers have all left, one by one. On the opposite side of the street the lights go out in a building. There's been talk of more raids to come. The sirens will wail and we'll hear the droning of the planes as they steer up-river. We're only waiting, people say.

*   *   *

Yesterday I imagined I was a guest at the fateful dinner party — and I wrote it all down, as if I was being inspired to, as if Pandora's lode was the spirit of the Muse secreted inside. I wrote it all down: about the violinist, the Right Honourable gentleman, the tipsy poet, the society hostess with scarlet nails like talons. I was there when the ceiling cracked and the first pieces of plaster tumbled. Fragments fell into the black Wedgwood plates of soup and when I looked up my fellow-guests' faces were bloodied, but they persevered notwithstanding. Elegantly I placed my elbows on the dining-table, laid with silver pheasants; I put my hands on my head and spread my fingers wide, to stop myself thinking, to cage all the diabolical thoughts I could feel pacing and stalking inside.

Then I tore up the pages. I flushed them down the water closet on the landing. Now their inky message is passing through the sewers of the city and I imagine my possession spreading everywhere like a contagion.

I notice the few people I pass in the streets staring at me — how I did to Mrs Drake/Darke — as if they're in dreadful awe of me.

These days I wear a lot of foundation and talcum and, on my cheeks, rouge. I like vivid shades of scarves and woollen mittens to wear — not blues, but brave yellows and reds — colours with a 'presence', and I always dress (mittens apart) as if for an occasion. I watch to check that my shadow travels with me, wherever I choose to go. I've taken to breathing freely on shop windows, between the latticework of black tape, mapping hot islands on the glass. I stop in my tracks and consider my breath puffing in front of me: like the brewers' drays that come clopping through Holborn, snorting their scuds of steam-train smoke.

* * *

One single light bulb burns above my table.

In *The Times* there's a notice in the 'Domestic Situations' column, in a box someone has ringed and underlined urgently with red ink, and I feel I have been here before, on the loop: it's advertising for the services of a young woman with 'proven secretarial abilities' to act as a lady's 'companion-cum-social secretary' in her new home.

I remind myself: we all of us 'serve', in our different ways.

A familiar telephone number is included but I have no more coins left in my purse to ring with.

* * *

I've heard it said that our life stories have already been written for us — and all we do is act them out.

This is a tale to be kept for night: when the moon shines in on a high-walled garden, or the wind sighs through an orchard of creaking boughs as ripe apples tumble into the long, whispering grass.

We're only waiting, they say.

I'm waiting with my story, my woof of words. Perhaps it's my fate, my end in life, that I sit here waiting.

What for? The sirens' call?

Whenever the black-out sounds, no one has the command to

black out the moon. She shines eerily and catches owls and hares in her track and turns the silver leaves on the new vegetation that has seeded in the rubble-flats.

I'm telling you of history. I'm telling you of these years that are conveniently termed our 'present' time, the 1940s. Days and nights of living on the edge.

In the time to come, beyond this dark one which will be forgotten, everything will have an explanation, I foresee. There will be no mysteries left, so people will convince themselves: at last, no more wonders.

Only . . .

It's down to waiting, they say, for what is to be: as if we're only ever in transit, like travellers passing time in a departure lounge.

Till these clouds of unknowing can part and the moon is shining freely in. Its argent light will cleave a track as bright and strong as daylight. Where it reaches is suddenly further than we have seen before, further and beyond: to the other side of what we call our here and now.